Partap Sharma is a pla...
of books for children. ...
Touch of Brightness ar...
Sumroo. Partap Sharma ...y ...ve ...en staged in
various countries and his books have been published
in India, England, USA, France, Denmark, Holland
and Canada. As an actor he has played the lead in
five Hindi feature films and won the National Award
in 1971 for his performance in *Phir Bhi*. Most
recently he has played the role of Nehru in the film
Nehru : The Jewel of India. He has directed a
number of documentary films, including a historical
series for Channel Four Television, London. His
voice is well-known to cinema, TV and radio
audiences, since he is one of India's foremost
commentators and narrators.

Dog Detective Ranjha

Partap Sharma

Rupa & Co

Copyright © Partap Sharma 1978

First published 1978 by Macmillan, London

Extract included in *Dog Stories* published by
Octopus Books (London) in 1981
Cathay Books (London) edition 1984

Indian comic strip of *Dog Detective Ranjha*
began in Tinkle magazine 1982

Indian paperback edition of *Dog Detective Ranjha*
published by India Book House 1984

First published by
Rupa in Paperback 1995
Second impression 1999

Published by
Rupa & Co
7/16, Ansari Road, Daryaganj, New Delhi 110 002
15 Bankim Chatterjee Street, Calcutta 700 073
135 South Malaka, Allahabad 211 001
P. G. Solanki Path, Lamington Road, Bombay 400 007

ISBN 81-7167-304-X

Printed in India by
Saurabh Print-O-Pack
A 15-16 Sector 4
Noida

The people of India love all animals. Some of the world's earliest animal stories were written in India. And even today the streets are open not only to traffic and human beings but also to friendly cows and bulls who wander freely as they please, sometimes absentmindedly standing in a bus queue or staring in with curiosity from the doorstep of a shop. There are even festivals for the less loved creatures, like snakes. Birds, of course, are often fed little morsels even by those who can hardly afford a daily meal for themselves. In the great epic, Mahabharata, *it is said that when the legendary hero, Yuddhister went to heaven he insisted that his dog should be allowed to accompany him.*

It is to such people all over the world who love animals that this book is dedicated.

Contents

1

Woof, Wuff and the Ways of Tughlak

*B*eing a detective dog is not easy. You have to be as good as a police dog and yet you have to be discreet. Also, you don't live in a kennel but in the house of your master with his family so you have always to be gentle, especially with the baby, and not even bark at a cat when the baby is asleep.

But before I tell you of the crimes I solved and the criminals I sent to jail, let me tell you how I became a working dog.

I didn't realise it at the time but my training began the moment I met my master.

He is a pleasant young man with a boyish face, a quick smile and a manner so casual it isn't always possible to make out whether he is joking or serious. He had come to the Brindia Kennels run by Mr and Mrs Tamhane in Bombay in order to buy an Alsatian pup, or more correctly a German Shepherd pup. So my sister and I were carried into the drawing room and introduced. We were about six weeks old then and were the only two left out of a litter of four. Two of my brothers had gone to their new homes the day before. Mrs Tamhane said that she had especially kept me back because I was her favourite. I don't know whether she really meant it or was saying it just to please Woof.

Woof is not his real name, of course, but that is what I called my master when I first saw him, and even now when I want to draw his attention I call out softly, "Woof!"

We were set down on the rug and my sister, Daisy, just flopped in a heap.

Woof muttered, "Her legs are weak."

He seemed to be ignoring me, so I started moving towards him.

"He walks like a drunkard," Woof chuckled.

Whatever he meant by that may have been funny but I felt sure it wasn't very polite. After all, I was doing my best. So I barked a few things back at him.

Barking vigorously at that age can be quite an effort. It made me recoil backwards and, without wanting to, I rolled over.

Woof started laughing, of course, but I was up in a second. Then he said a very lovely thing.

"Mrs Tamhane," he said, "please bring a bowl of milk and bread. I'd like to see them eat. I suppose, of course, that they've been properly weaned and can now do without their mother's milk."

When the bowl was brought and we had taken a quick little gobble of the soggy bread, he pulled the bowl away and placed it behind us. Daisy was bewildered and just flopped down again. I thought Woof was being cruel and I decided I wasn't going to let him succeed in hiding the food. So I sniffed and, yes, from over there behind me came the delicious aroma of milk and bread. I turned and went to the bowl.

Woof said, "He'll be a good tracker. I'll take him."

That was the first time I had heard the word *tracker* and it seemed an odd thing to say.

"Are you with the police then?" Mrs Tamhane asked.

Woof shook his head, smiled and, without another word,

wrote out a cheque and handed it to her.

She glanced at the signature and exclaimed, "But, of course, I've heard of you—you're one of our young writers! No wonder you look familiar. I've seen you on television, reading out some of your works." Then her voice took on a puzzled tone. "But I still don't understand. Why do you want to train him to be a tracker?"

Woof seemed at a loss to answer. He fumbled about. At last, he said simply, "It's a . . . childhood dream of mine. I've always dreamt of a highly capable dog in the house, a sort of fantastic animal companion to the family."

"Oh," said Mrs Tamhane as she picked up the bowl which I had by now licked clean. Then she sighed and said, "Good luck!"

I thought I'd find out more about this Woof. He seemed a strange sort of fellow. So I wobbled carefully towards him and took a good sniff at his shoes and trousers. The scent of his body was pleasing and I think my tail must have wagged. Now that is one of the awful things about being a dog—you can't help showing your feelings.

Woof was delighted. He picked me off the floor and petted me and said, "I'm glad you're friendly. What a glossy black coat you have and what beautiful markings! You'll be quite a handsome dog."

"Oh yes," Mrs Tamhane agreed, "he's bound to win a few prizes. After all, he comes from a family of show dogs. Both his parents are champions. The Sydenberg line is good looking and intelligent."

"I'm not really interested in showing dogs," Woof said, "fact is, I've never been to a dog show in my life. And I don't really care about pedigree. I want to train him to be a working dog, so that he can be of some help to people."

Mrs Tamhane looked quizzically at Woof, and Woof just shrugged and laughed.

Then she said, "Ah yes, I almost forgot—your childhood dream."

Woof grinned in an embarrassed sort of way and started moving to the door, with me in his arms. I could see that I would have to spend a great deal of time looking after him. Though he was a family man with a wife and a baby, it was plain that he was still quite a child at heart, still quite a dreamer.

In the car I began to froth and foam and was sick.

Woof really knew very little about dogs then, because he thought I had some horrible disease. He wanted to rush me back to the Tamhanes or even have me put to sleep at once! But by now we had collected his wife, Wuff, from the bazaar where she had been shopping and she turned out to be far more sensible about such things. After all, she was a mother.

She said to Woof, "I think the poor mite has just had too much milk and bread. And this is the first time he's been in a car. It must be terrifying for him."

Thank heavens she was there!

But you see what I mean? You not only have to adjust to the strange world of human beings, you also have to be prepared to be mis-diagnosed and misunderstood. I tell you, you need patience with human beings.

As a puppy, I had more lessons in patience than I can describe. The baby pulled my tail, patted me so that I tottered and fell, pinched my nose, examined my teeth, poked my ribs, tugged at my ears and hugged me so that I wanted to howl aloud.

Fortunately for my sake, Woof and Wuff never left me alone with the baby. She would have killed me with love.

I've now come to the conclusion that human beings also need to be trained so that they learn to live with other animals.

A city dog has to adjust from the moment he is born. And to be born in the heart of Bombay is very different from being born in, say, some quiet little village in the cool of the Himalayas.

For that matter, Wuff must have had to adjust a great deal. You see, she's English and grew up in the chilly, damp climate of England. Woof, of course, is Indian but even he is not quite used to the heat because he comes from the colder regions of the North. That perhaps is why he takes every opportunity to go up into the hills to write. The weather there is wonderfully bracing.

Bombay has a warm, sticky climate and the only time a puppy feels like frisking about is early in the morning or late in the evening when the sun is low on the horizon. The rest of the time any sensible pup would just want to sleep. But imagine the noise that millions of people on the streets can make, with their buying and selling, their talking and singing, their shouting and laughing. Then add to that the sounds of cars and buses, trains and horses, policemen's whistles and bicycle bells. At first I was constantly alarmed and wondered how human beings could put up with it. I saw that, night or afternoon, some people just slept through it all!

It was Tughlak, the old black Labrador living with the Pandits nearby, who first explained it to me.

He said, "Son, take it easy, relax. You're far too jumpy and alert. All of you can't be on duty all the time. You've got to let half of you rest sometime."

"I don't understand, sir," I whined and sniffed his nose once just to make sure he wasn't ill or slightly crackers or anything.

"Look at you," he growled as he lay under his master's chair. "Here you are at a party with your humans. Everyone's enjoying himself and yet you keep looking over your shoulder as though you'd lost your tail. You're as frightened and fidgety as a cat!"

A pup learns to take an insult or two from his elders. I did the ritual thing. I wagged my behind, lowered myself on to my belly and grovelled a little.

"Guru," I said, "please explain it to me."

"Guru! Nothing doing, boy," he snapped. "I'm no guru and I'm no fool. Don't try and work those clever-clever tricks on me. I may be a Pandit but I'm not traditional. I eat beef."

"I'm sorry, uncle—" I began, but he cut me short with a low snarl.

"Uncle, funckle, nothing, boy! Just be straight with me. That's how I like it. Call me Tughlak. That's my name. Now, let me tell you what the trouble is with you. You don't realise that we dogs hear nine or ten times better than human beings."

"Really?" I said.

"Of course. Humans don't have their senses as well-developed as we dogs. Right now, for instance, all they can hear are the noises of this party and only the deeper sounds at that. But we can hear that horrible squeak as the tap is turned on in the bathroom and, see that fellow there opening the soda-bottle—"

"Yes," I whispered. "Gosh! What a terrible screech and a pop."

"Well, boy," said Tughlak licking his lips with satisfaction, "all they can hear is the pop."

"No!" I said. It was astounding.

"And," Tughlak drawled as he yawned, "they can't even hear that car five hundred yards away and they didn't hear that plane going by overhead. They have a word for that kind of plane, boy. They call it supersonic. But . . ." he gave a short laugh and let it go at that while the corner of his mouth twitched in a sneer.

Just then I pricked up my ears.

"Easy, boy, easy," Tughlak growled. "That whistle you heard came from the street. It's not your master calling. You see, you've got to learn to distinguish. And that way you'll be able to relax."

"Thank you, sir," I said.

It was still difficult for me to call him just Tughlak.

Some people would say I was missing out on a great deal, not having a kennel to myself. But the way I looked at it was that Woof's entire flat was my kennel and that was a generous enough kennel for any dog to have.

Of course, right from the beginning, it meant putting up with humans and respecting their customs. It meant, to use their phrase, being "house-broken". It annoyed them if I made a mess

on the floor. At first I was bewildered and thought they preferred me to use the carpet. But after I did that, I found they had washed that spot and it didn't smell quite right for a repeat performance. Just as I was getting anxious and sniffing around for some place that could be my permanent bathroom, Woof picked me up and rushed outside and set me down in a corner of the garden. I didn't want to spoil the clean sand and the lovely grass. Woof kept saying something that sounded to me as if he was imitating a bird.

"Do it, do it, do it," he said.

I ignored him and sniffed around and, to my surprise, I could smell other dogs on the hedges and shrubs. I padded about from bush to bush and it was like coming into a room with signatures scrawled on the walls. Every dog of the area seemed to have left his 'I-was-here' mark.

Now, as a puppy you don't want to get into trouble with bigger dogs about which place belongs to whom. So I chose a sort of virgin spot and let go with my 'I-was-here.'

In the days to come, I learnt to let Woof know whenever I felt uncomfortable and out we would go and Woof would put me down and make his bird sounds and I would bomb the target.

Now it's much simpler.

Woof just has to say, "Do it," and, whosever bush it is, by golly, I do it.

Tughlak began to play a bit of a part in my life. We kept bumping into him everywhere.

His master, Gokul Pandit, would bring him to the racecourse in the evening. The racecourse is the only open expanse of ground in that part of Bombay where a dog can freely exercise himself—that is, when the horse-races are not on.

Even at the racecourse, Tughlak never lost his sense of dignity. No running or scampering about like me. No, sir, he would lumber out and wait for his collar to be adjusted and the chain to be unknotted and then he would walk slowly but powerfully in the direction he wished. Gokul often tried to walk with us but Tughlak took him off the other way. That was Tughlak all over—totally independent.

Then we would bump into them coming round from the opposite direction. Tughlak would stop and Gokul would quickly think of some conversation to begin with Woof.

Usually Woof would say, "Let him off, Gokul. Let him play with Ranjha."

And Gokul would say, "Oh, he's too old to play."

Just then Tughlak would wag his tail and lunge at me, unbalancing Gokul on his feet. Tughlak was like that, independent and a little perverse.

One day Gokul presented me with a very smart red leather collar and leash that had been made just for me. I was delighted. But Tughlak, who was off the chain, trotted me off to a corner and said, "Chew it up, boy, chew it up."

"Oh no," I said. "It's lovely. And Woof scolds me if I chew up things."

"Suit yourself, boy. I chew up anything I can. Got to show them who's boss. Can't bear a collar and leash of dried skin hanging from my neck. Eat it up. Best thing to do."

"It's a matter of taste," I said.

"You said it, boy, you said it!" Tughlak smacked his lips.

"I mean," I insisted, "I prefer to be on a leather leash. That way, in an emergency, I could get free whereas with a chain—"

"Ah, of course," said Tughlak looking down and absentmindedly pawing a tuft of grass. "You're being brought up as a police dog or something, aren't you?"

"Well, yes and no," I admitted.

"Be straight, boy, be straight with me. What do you mean—yes and no?"

"Well, I'm being trained like a police dog but I've got to be a private detective."

"Never heard of such a thing."

"Let me put it this way. I'll work on a police case if they ask for me but I'll always stay with Woof. I'm Woof's dog, and Wuff's and the baby's. I'm a family dog first and a crime-solver after."

"Hm, hm," he muttered. Then he threw up a shower of sand with his hindlegs and snorted. "These new-fangled ideas!"

But a few days later he said exactly the opposite.

"Nothing new in these ideas, boy. Why, it's just a channelling of all the old things our forefathers did as wild dogs in the jungles. Tracking is like being on the scent of game. It's a part of hunting. Retrieving is like what we did for our young ones—bringing back food for them to eat. Arresting is like holding a wild beast at bay. And attacking—humph, why any dog can do that."

"Maybe," I said. "But the difference in being trained is that you understand when to start and when to stop and when to be still."

He thought that out for a while, then he said something very peculiar.

"A bit like Zen," he said and, nodding, walked away.

I realised then that though I may become a mystery-solver I could never hope to fully puzzle out the ways of Tughlak.

Tughlak could never remember my name. In fact, he could hardly remember anything except his own name. He had once asked me to explain why I was called Ranjha. I had told him that I was named after the dashing young hero of a famous folk-opera of Punjab.

"Ah," said Tughlak. "So if you were living in Europe, you might be called Romeo."

"Perhaps," I agreed.

"But," he growled, "you don't look like any kind of Romeo to me. You're handsome all right. That I'll grant you. You're good looking but as for being any kind of Casanova—"

"No, no," I interrupted. "The name is Ranjha."

"What difference?" he snorted. "Ranjha, Romeo, Casanova!

It's all the same thing. Now take my name—Tughlak. I'm named after a sultan, a king. Do you think I look anything like a king?"

It was a tricky question. I whined and said, "Of course you *do* have a majestic manner . . ."

Tughlak said, "Hm . . . hm . . ." then grunted and belched. I could see he was flattered. Nevertheless, the fact remained that he considered all names pointless and useless. He had three standard ways of addressing any dog he met. Little bitches were called "kiddo", male pups "boy" and adult dogs "Old Toot". Tughlak was altogether very modern. He spoke only English.

I was being trained in Hindi, the national language of India. Tughlak found that odd. And I suppose it was odd. Somehow even in India, everyone always spoke to dogs in English. But Woof had his own ideas. He didn't want anyone to confuse me by being able to give me commands. So he decided to train me in Hindi.

One of the first words I learnt to obey was *nahin* meaning "no". But Tughlak didn't always remember what "no" meant.

We would be walking about the racecourse and along would come a dainty young Poodle and off Tughlak would go with his master yelling, "No, no, no!"

Tughlak had an eye for dainty young Poodles. They reminded him of his youth. He told me that he had once been in love with a Poodle but she had despised him for being "a hulking big brute" and, though she was fluent in English, she had snapped back at him in French and tried to throw him off her scent. But he never gave up trying. Eventually her mistress stopped bringing her to the racecourse and Tughlak went through life chasing the ghost of his first love.

At such moments life became quite chaotic for his master, and the air would grow heavy with apologies. I, on the other hand, would stop dead when my master said, "Ranjha, no!"

Tughlak would be brought back, contrite and ashamed. He would see that I was concerned at the way he sometimes forgot himself and lost control and all his usual dignity. Then he would say mournfully, "You don't understand, boy. You haven't got the same incentive. You're growing up. You're now four months old. But you're still a pup. You haven't got the same incentive."

"It's not only that," I would say, since I didn't like being reminded that I wasn't a grown-up. "It's also that I have this choke-chain collar round my neck."

He would examine it, and I would explain all over again how it tightened punishingly round my neck if I tried to run away.

"Hm, hm," he said. "I'm sorry your master is so cruel to you."

"Oh, he's not," I said. "You see, it doesn't bother me at all if I don't misbehave. And this way I learn to walk at heel and watch my master's every step."

"Walk at heel?" Tughlak said. "What is that?"

"Why, I walk on the left side of my master and when he stops I sit and when he walks I keep pace with him—neither faster nor slower."

"Humph," Tughlak muttered, "and all because you have that silly slip-chain round your neck!"

"Not at all," I said proudly. "I can do it without the collar and the leash. That's called *heeling free*. My master has only to give the word and slap his left thigh and wherever I am, I come running to his left side and do as he does."

Tughlak was not impressed. He grunted, belched and said, "What a lot of useless humbug!"

But a few days later an incident took place that made him change his mind.

In the centre of the racecourse is a large meadow and at the far end of it is a polo field. That evening there was a polo match in progress and dog-owners naturally kept carefully away from that end.

Tughlak and I were wandering free, nosing about among the flowers and grass when suddenly a pony which had thrown her rider came thundering across the meadow. We were directly in her path.

Woof didn't panic but shouted to me clearly, "Ranjha, heel!"

And I went running straight to his side.

But Tughlak looked up and saw this monster tearing down at him. He could hear his master shouting, "Tughlak, Tughlak!" But he didn't know what he was supposed to do. Was it a command to attack this monster because it was a danger to his master or should he run from it? Tughlak was undecided. The pony, with her ears back and the whites of her eyes showing, made Tughlak the focus of her fear. She reared up with the stirrups flying and the bit clacking between her teeth and gave a terrifying neigh. Tughlak danced about before her as though he was on hot bricks. The pony wanted to run and Tughlak was in her way. She brought her forelegs down and drumming the earth furiously, she charged.

Now Tughlak didn't need any command. He cowered, turned, and ran. The pony was bolting and old Tughlak was racing to keep ahead of her.

I must confess I had a desire to help poor Tughlak. I wanted to chase the pony and hang on to her tail. Later, when I told Tughlak this, he said, "That's what our forefathers would have done. And we would have killed the pony and eaten it, too. But the world of humans is different. They keep the funniest pets."

But alone, Tughlak was no match for the pony. He veered from left to right and finally took cover behind a mounting platform. The pony went tearing past.

When we reached Tughlak he was quivering like a jelly and could hardly stand up.

"I'll take him home," Gokul said.

But before Gokul could put him on his chain, Tughlak, too, had the same idea and dashed for the safety of the car.

Now there is a little road that separates the turf from the parking lot and Tughlak, untrained in using his senses, crossed without looking left and right.

A van was taking off after the pony and Tughlak was in the centre of the road. Of course, his master shouted. This time Tughlak stopped but he neither went forward nor came back to heel. There was a terrible screeching of brakes. The van swerved and one fender hit Tughlak on the rear. He was flung aside.

The driver was cursing and he waved a fist at Gokul but Gokul shrugged and, for the hundredth time apologized and the driver swung on the wheel and roared off after the pony.

Tughlak collected himself and sitting up dazedly, stayed where he was.

His master scolded him and massaged him and petted him. Woof also looked to see if he was all right. Apart from a bit of shock, Tughlak was the same.

Well, not quite the same. A new realization seemed to have been knocked into him. As I licked his face and tried to revive him, he cocked one eye and said, "I've been enlightened, boy, enlightened. You've got something there, with all that business of going to heel. It's the middle way between life and death."

2

Up in the Hills and the Ways of Woof

The family and I went up to Mahabaleshwar in the hills for four months. It was a working holiday. Woof was writing a novel and I was training to be a detective.

I would get my lessons every morning and evening when we went for our walks. The rest of the time Woof would be busy at his desk. But actually I was so keen to become a full-fledged detective that I kept in training all the time. Perhaps I was a little over-eager. I sniffed out squirrels, jumped over flower-beds, ran up and down the steps—you never know what a detective might not have to do when after his quarry. I investigated every nook and corner of the big house we had rented and carried out all suspicious-looking objects such as slippers, socks and half-used pencils. Once, I felt sure there was something hiding inside a cushion. Of course, I didn't sniff to make certain. Had I done so I would have known at once that there was nothing there except stuffing. It was just a hunch, and I played the hunch. I gnawed at the cushion, worried it all over the floor and managed to rip it

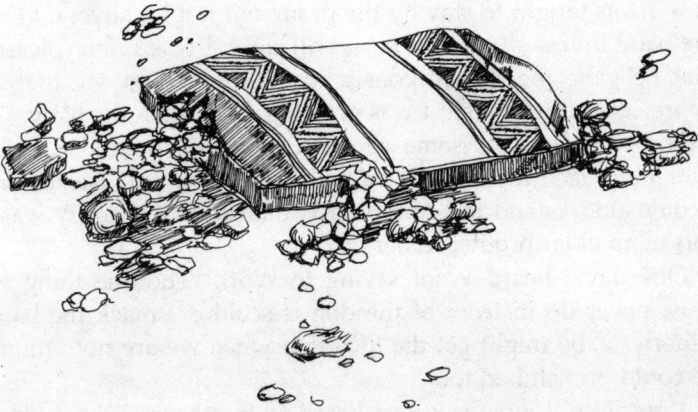

apart, just to check.

That began the distaff side of my training. I was scolded, smacked on the bottom and made to sit quietly in a corner.

It was Wuff who was more angry than Woof and it was she who always dealt a little more firmly with me. Woof is a bit of a softie. I only have to whine, put my ears back and my head between my paws and he will pet and console me—if Wuff isn't looking. She believes absolutely in the value of punishment; he believes in good deeds followed by reward. Between them they taught me to distinguish right from wrong.

Though Wuff was harder with me sometimes, I saw right from the start that she needed my protection more. Most of all, of course, I realised that the baby was a helpless dithering thing that padded about smiling and gurgling, ready to trust any stranger. So I naturally began to take particular care of the baby and Wuff.

I had learnt to sit and lie down on command—and Woof always rewarded me with a little titbit if I did these right—and now I was taught to stay by the pram and not let anyone touch the baby unless Woof said it was all right. I was rather pleased that he gave me this responsibility. Also, I could see that he appreciated the fact that I was growing faster than the baby. We were both about the same age—six months now—but I could run, jump, feed myself, carry a newspaper or a little basket, and I could understand far more words than she. So I really was a sort of an elder brother to her.

One day I heard Woof saying to Wuff, "The one thing we must never do in front of the dog is scold or smack the baby. Otherwise, he might get the idea that when we are not around, he could punish her, too."

Very wise, I must say. I've heard from other dogs how their intentions were often mistaken and they were beaten, and how some others had even been put to sleep forever for only doing what they had so often seen their master and mistress do.

I was taught to take any kind of misbehaviour by the baby

and not to even take her hand in my mouth the way I might with Woof or Wuff.

But all this came more or less naturally to me—I didn't really need to be taught to love the baby.

My real training took place during our walks. Mahabaleshwar has lovely wooded paths and clearings. In these clearings, I was taught to retrieve. Woof would throw something—a bone, a ball, a stick—and I was expected to bring it back. At first I didn't quite understand what I was to do. I would chase after the object all right but I didn't always bring it back to him. I often just ran about with it and expected Woof to chase me for it. I had seen other dogs do that and I thought it would be fun. But Woof refused to chase me. He just stood there with a piece of meat or a bit of biscuit in his hand waiting for me to bring the object to him. Sometimes, of course, the temptation of the reward made me go straight up to him and deliver the object. Then he would reward me and pet me. Soon his petting became enough reward for me. But, I must confess, I wasn't always inclined to go straight back to him. I felt he was taking it too easy, he wasn't working for his reward the way I was, so I sometimes just carried the object off here and there and worried it. Then Woof would start walking in the opposite direction and I would scamper after him thinking he was going to leave me behind—but when I was abreast of him he would bend down and take the object from me. I knew I had been tricked. After a few times of this, I decided to be cleverer and I would simply follow at a safe distance. If he called me to heel, I would drop the object before going to him. Then he did a very cunning thing indeed.

He put the choke-collar on me and tied a long length of cord to it. When he next threw a stick for me I went off after it not realising that this length of cord was rolling out behind me.

I picked up the stick but the moment I began to run away with it, he began reeling me in gently as though I were a fish.

A few times of this and I decided that it was best to return the stick to him and get on with something else which was more fun.

But little did I realise what fun retrieving can be—if you have to *find* the object. Just picking up a stick or ball and bringing it back is no challenge to an intelligent dog but choosing the right object to carry back *is*. And step by step, Woof was leading me to it.

Now, on our walks, he would pick up a twig much like any other and rub his hands on it. Then, holding me by the collar, he would throw the twig into the woods so that it was lost among the numerous twigs on the ground. Then he would give me the scent of his hands by cupping his palms over my nose and with the command, "Seek-Fetch!" he would let me off.

Into the woods I would go, scrambling through bramble and bush, sniffing the leaves and twigs. Then bang!

It would go tingling right up my nostrils—the scent of Woof's hands. But where did it come from now? *Sniff, sniff, sniff.* Not here, not there. Not this, not that. And—ah!—I would have it, one particular twig out of all those twigs and leaves.

Soon I was easily sniffing out twigs with Wuff's scent on them too, and then, of course, Woof began asking strangers to help. They were all quite interested to do so, so I began taking one sniff of a stranger's hand or his handkerchief and off I would go to bring back the object he had thrown.

The woods of Mahabaleshwar are full of the most fascinating smells. There are the fragrances of all the different flowers and leaves and trees. There are the smells of the ponies and the buffaloes and cows and the men who walk with them. There are the droppings of guinea fowl and pheasant and all kinds of birds. There are the sudden strange odours of wild boar and hare and the swift, sly panther. Here a snake stopped to sun itself; there a band of merry monkeys loped across.

On the banks of the lake, where you may always see holiday-makers rowing in boats, you get whiffs of fish and moss and water-weeds. On the quieter jungle side where few people go, you can make out the scent and tracks of hyenas that came the night before. And by the rivers you can smell out the spots used

by washerwomen to soap the clothes. The troupe of woodcutters and their women who walk single-file through the jungle leave their own trails—one perfume mingling and winding upon another odour, one aroma of food carried in a bag merging with another of tobacco in a pouch. And the body-scents are quite fantastic and quite individual. No two human beings smell alike. Their clothes, their shoes, the food they eat, the liquor they may have had or the things they smoke and chew—each of these combine with their state of health to make the body-scent unique.

Learning to make full use of my ability to sniff out and track was an exhilarating and overpowering experience. I often felt the blood rush up to my head and my nostrils quivering and sometimes I felt the excitement was so strong that I would collapse if I didn't rush forward to the end of the trail. Sometimes the sheer joy of advancing on a track with the scent growing stronger so filled my being that I thought I would burst like a balloon. If I went on for miles, it exhausted me. I would have to lie down then and rest and I would feel oh so thirsty!

Then I would remember Tughlak's advice and relax.

When we were in Mahabaleshwar I often thought of Tughlak and looked forward to surprising him with my new skills but, of course, Tughlak never would admit to being impressed. He liked to take everything in his stride. Yet I knew that he was proud to have me as his friend.

"So you can track now," he said to me when we got back. "So what? It's nothing new, except to you. Dogs have done it before. In fact, only dogs can do it this well. Humans can't."

"Really?" I said. "You mean they don't feel their senses being jostled and bothered by this riot of smells?"

Tughlak laughed. He seemed to know everything though he couldn't do anything. As I became more educated, I realised that Tughlak was, as they say, an academic, an intellectual, a theoretician.

He said, "Humans can't smell beyond their noses. Our nostrils are long, with very sensitive membranes, and we can trace the origin of a smell that is many days old. But again, boy, you've got to distinguish and discriminate. Otherwise, you'll go crazy, you'll go beserk, wallowing in millions of smells at the same time."

I just happened then to sniff at a butterfly flitting by.

Tughlak said, "Forget it. Ignore that butterfly. You can neither eat it nor will your master ever ask you to track it. Choose and then concentrate. That is what makes a good working dog."

I nodded.

But Tughlak had not finished. He said, "I know what you're thinking, boy. You're thinking: what does this fat old fogey know—"

"No, no," I protested.

"Another thing, boy," Tughlak grumbled. "Dogs don't lie. They can't. So don't even bother to try. That's why humans trust us. They know we are honest and straightforward. They depend on us more than they can on most other humans. So, boy, I'm a fat old fogey. I can't do a quarter of the things you can. And I won't have a tenth of the adventures you will. But between eating and sleeping, boy, I *think*, I'm a thinker. And don't you forget that, boy."

Tughlak scratched at a tick that was trying to make itself at home in his coat. I wagged my tail and waited. Tughlak had a lot he wanted to get off his chest. As he grew older, he was getting more pompous. But I had learnt to be patient. Why, I could sit and stay for half an hour in one place if my master commanded me to do so. So I waited for Tughlak to have his say.

"Now most humans," he said, "believe that we don't think at all. I mean, they think they are the only animals that think."

"Come, come, sir," I yelped, unable to stay quiet at that. "My Woof knows I think. If I didn't, how could I even begin to understand what he wants me to do?"

"Exactly," Tughlak said. "But, as I've told you before, their senses are limited. To make up for that they have developed this grand idea of themselves. They truly believe that they are the only animals that think."

"Incredible!" I cried.

"Quite," Tughlak nodded. Then he lay down and rolling on to his back looked thoughtfully up at the sky. "The fact of the matter is that they think *better* than other animals because they are gifted with a better *memory*. They can remember what two plus two is. But we can't. If you asked me now, I couldn't tell you. At best we depend on instinct and on habit or training. They just remember. Now if we could remember a basic thing like two plus two, we could go on to higher things. But we can't."

"Just a minute," I said. "I'm not sure you're quite right. I often remember things that Woof doesn't. I remember the smell of a man I tracked long ago. I remember a spot where I picked up an object two weeks back because a hint of the smell is still there."

"That's different," Tughlak said, sitting up. "That's different because it's not that humans forget such things; they just don't know. It comes back to the same thing—most of their senses are limited."

My tracking lessons had begun with Woof laying trails about the house with the little bits of boiled meat. That was easy work.

Then he took me out to a group of strangers. He made me take the scent of one of them, then he sent me off to retrieve that man's handkerchief from among a number that were on the ground. That was easy too. I had already done this with the bits of wood and twigs.

Then one morning I realised that something new was afoot. Woof tried to put a harness on me. It was too big, and one of the men standing about said, "He's only a puppy yet. You're teaching him much too early."

Woof said, "It's never too early to learn."

He put the harness aside and with some webbing he improvised a harness for me. It went comfortably round my neck and around my belly and was tied in a knot on my back, then it extended for many feet. Woof could now hold on to it and follow me. It took me some time to realise that I was expected to lead him and that he couldn't smell the scent that I was smelling.

No sooner was I snugly in the harness than a startling event took place which set me off on my first man-track. It must have all been pre-arranged to make me interested in giving chase, but all I understood then was that a huge, hulking brute of a man leapt out of some bushes with a stick in his hand and tried to attack Woof.

Immediately concerned for my master, I jumped snarling at the man. But Woof had a firm grip on the harness and I was held back.

The man now made threatening gestures with his stick and as he circled about I stood between him and Woof, barking and snapping at him to stay away if he valued his skin.

Then suddenly, to my surprise, the man turned on his heels and ran away. I strained at the harness but Woof wouldn't let me go. I wanted very much to catch the man; it was quite frustrating. However, I felt relieved that I had managed to frighten him away.

But that was not all. By this time the attacker had run beyond the bushes, out of sight. Woof now pointed to the ground and said, "Track."

The moment I put my nose down, I caught the attacker's scent and, by golly, I wanted to catch him! So we set off. I didn't even realise that I was already tracking!

We went down a path and I was just running on when I realised that the attacker's scent had gone. It wasn't there anymore. I turned in a short circle and—wham!—there it was again, clinging to the blades of grass and the thistles and twigs. I was so anxious now that I couldn't help giving a low moaning cry; now I know that it is a cry that comes to me only when I am hot on the trail. So I gave this cry—which is not quite a bark, not quite a yelp, not quite a groan—and I set off into the bushes with Woof holding on to the long lead of the harness and following

about two yards behind.

The scent was very strong now. It was like following the smell of food and suddenly finding your nose in the hot cooking pot. There he was! He stood there with the stick upraised and I barked at him but again I was held back by Woof. Then just as the man swung the stick down, Woof shouted, "Disarm," and gave me some play on the lead.

I naturally jumped and caught the stick and wrenched it out of the man's hand. The man suddenly seemed to become very timid and he just stood there quietly.

Now Woof said to me, "Ranjha, drop it." This is what he says when I have retrieved something and he wants me to deliver it, so I gave Woof the stick. Then he said, "Ranjha, sit, stay."

I wanted to jump at the man but Woof repeated the command firmly and I obeyed. After all, Woof is my master.

Then Woof reached into a plastic bag which he took out of his pocket and he gave me a delicious titbit to eat. I was glad he appreciated my work.

Then to my surprise he went up to the attacker and began to chat calmly. They were behaving like old friends. I was bewildered. Woof put an arm round the man's shoulder and patting him said clearly, "All right. Friend."

The man started to walk away and I half-rose to stop him. But Woof said, "Ranjha, no! Sit, stay." And after a while he repeated, "All right. Friend."

The man had by now walked away. Woof petted me profusely and hugged me and kept saying, "Good dog, Ranjha. Good dog." He was very, very pleased with me. I was delighted. I licked his hands and face and wagged my tail and we celebrated our first successful track.

Later, when I told him about all this, Tughlak said, "Of course, of course. Your human is right. Even more important than catching a criminal is being able to let an innocent man go. And neither should ever be hurt, eh boy? Unless they intend to cause hurt. It all points to some deeply thought out philosophy, boy. And I intend to get to the bottom of it all. I'm thinking, boy, I'm thinking. Just give me a little more time and I'll have it all worked out. But I tell you, it's fascinating—this world of humans."

3

The Case of the Sudden Killer

*T*ughlak was right. The world of humans was fascinating. But it could be frightening too. It was when we were back in Bombay for a short spell that I solved my first case. And I can tell you it was frightening—because I was far from ready to take on such a task. I was a pup of seven months with one of my ears still floppy and my legs splaying slightly in front and hocking at the back. I may have looked cuddly and loveable but no working dog worth his bone considers that enough qualification. I knew I was still a mere novice. I didn't yet have enough confidence and I was not big enough to take care of myself. I was only knee-high to a man.

That is why it gave me the jitters to hear from Tughlak that there was an attacker on the loose.

Tughlak's eyes were rimmed red with worry. He said, "You've come back to the city at a wrong time, boy. There's a madman on the loose. He goes about killing dogs. He prowls about the Warden Road area at dusk and his *modus operandi* is to attack suddenly with a huge block of stone. The dog's head is crushed. Death is instantaneous. No one knows why he does it.

The humans are worried and are trying to trap him but he always manages to run away before anyone can see his face. Jowlie is dead, Rani is dead, Pookie is dead. Of course, they were what are called stray dogs, but two days ago Grumpy, the old Boxer, was killed on the Breachcandy sea front while his master was looking for crabs among the rocks. And last night Junker, the Doberman Pinscher, was done in while innocently examining a lamp-post."

"Junker!" I exclaimed. "But that's impossible. He could jump walls five feet high, he could run like a deer and he was a big enough to settle any attacker."

"True, true," Tughlak said sadly, with a little sniffling sound. "But he was not trained to be alert and he was so humanized that he trusted even strangers."

"Poor Junker," I said and I could feel my own legs trembling and quivering. I went to a nearby bush and did the needful.

"But don't you worry too much, boy," Tughlak advised. "Just stick close to your master. Life in the city is not safe anymore."

A couple of days after that I almost died at the hands of the sudden attacker.

My master's flat was on the ground floor and, since we had been away for a month, the study had been taken over by a club of neighbourhood cats. They would hold their meetings in the study at night, coming in through the open windows and bringing with them whatever smelly snacks they wished to devour in peace.

"Oof! What a terrible stink!" said Woof when we first came in. Of course, I knew at once that cats had been about but Woof thought there might be a dead mouse somewhere so he gave me the order to search.

I poked about and drew out all the fishbones and scraps the cats had left behind. Woof examined the evidence and muttered, "These damned crows! Flying in through the windows."

I couldn't blame him for coming to the wrong conclusion. The crows of the area are quite naughty and venturesome and it's not at all unlike them to flit in and out of people's houses if no one is around.

I decided to keep my information to myself for the time being and to catch at least one of the culprits the next evening. If they had got away with trespassing for so long I deduced that they were bound to try it again.

Sure enough, the next night they came—creeping in silently through the window grills. Even the grey tabby with the little bell round her neck made no noise. She lowered herself so carefully from the ledge that there was not a tinkle. I must say I admired their stealth.

But my nose didn't fail me. The moment I received a whiff of unwashed cats, I raised my hackles and brought my tail up to an angle of warning. Then I went to Woof who was reading in bed and nudged him the way I had been taught. We had to be as quiet as the intruders. The baby was asleep.

Woof put on his slippers and followed me to the study. The moment he put on the light, there was a flurry of cats and they darted miaowing and yowling for the windows.

Now Woof is an animal-lover which means that he even loves cats, and he has trained me not to run after anything unless he gives the command. But he wanted to teach the cats a lesson and he gave me the command, "Catch." I sprang after the tabby.

In her panic the tabby slipped and fell back from the window, but—as happen with all cats—she landed on her feet. Crouching before me she bared her teeth and spat and her tail shot up as though it had an electric current in it. I barked and looked for an opening in her defence.

Just then Wuff came in and said, "What's all this noise?"

In that second's distraction, the tabby jumped up to the ledge and was out of the grill.

"Catch him!" Woof said again and opened the door. I shot off after the cat with Woof running behind me. He wanted to really scare the cat so it wouldn't come into his study again.

The cat sped off behind the next block, skirting flower-pots

and dustbins, trying to jump up on to a wall. But I wasn't going to give her enough time to spring.

In the excitement of the chase I quite forgot about the sudden killer of Warden Road. And that's when I was attacked.

We were now behind another building and at the end of its cluttered backyard was the shack of a *dhobi* who laundered clothes for the residents of the place. The cat rushed into the *dhobi*'s shack. Outside, by a heap of rubbish and stones, was a young man taking the air. He seemed just another good human and both the cat and I zipped past him without a second thought.

The cat found herself cornered in the shack and leaping over the ironing-board and waking the poor *dhobi* who was asleep, she jumped clear over my head and was out again, running back along the wall. I swung round and after her.

But now the killer by the rubbish mound had picked up a huge block of stone.

As I came out I saw him raise it over his head. Woof, too, had seen him from a distance but had not realised his intention. I was running beside the wall when the killer, standing almost directly over me, flung the stone.

It smashed down on me, flattening me to the ground and I was aware of a terrible pain in my stomach as I yelped and my head swam with shock. I could hear Woof yelling at the killer and running towards him. And I heard the killer give a startled gasp, for he had not realised that Woof was nearby. The killer's footwear made a peculiar squeaking sound as he turned on his heel and raced away.

The buildings, the wall, the earth seemed to be heaving around me.

I tried to crawl out from under the stone but it was too much effort and I fainted.

When I came to, Woof was massaging my legs and feeling my stomach. A number of people were standing round commiserating and trying to help.

One of them brought a pan of water. Woof asked me to drink and I stood up shakily and lapped at the cool refreshing water.

There was the block of jagged stone. It wasn't a nightmare. It was real. Fortunately, the corner made by the wall and the ground had saved me. I had only been dazed. Had the killer thrown the stone a second earlier, I would almost certainly have died.

Woof hadn't heard of the killer before. Now the people standing about told him how every evening someone seemed to be going about killing dogs.

Woof said, "I thought it was a cat-lover trying to help the cat but I couldn't understand why he ran away."

"He was frightened he would be caught," someone said. "He must be slightly mad."

"Well," said Woof, "we must catch him, then." And I sensed Woof's voice changing from bewilderment to anger.

No one knew who the man was nor could anyone give even a rough description of him. The *dhobi* said that he had been aware of someone standing outside his shack but he had kept his eyes shut because he didn't want anyone asking him to iron clothes at that hour of night.

"All right," Woof said, petting me and making sure I was able to walk, "we'll track him. Even if Ranjha dies later due to some internal injury, at least he will know the culprit has not escaped."

One of the men gladly went and fetched the tracking harness from Wuff and I was strapped in.

What we did next was something a little beyond my training at that stage. Till then I had always taken the scent from a piece of cloth or some object; now I had to take it from a general direction!

Woof had seen which way the killer ran. Now he pointed me in that direction and walked me forward with the command, "Scent. Track."

My head was spinning and I stumbled a little. But then I caught the scent of a man and I knew it was the scent I had crossed when I was after the cat. I knew it was the scent of the killer.

I set off and Woof urged me on gently but I hardly needed any urging now. Behind us the crowd of residents grew. They were amazed. They had never seen such a thing before. They discussed it loudly and tried to question Woof about my abilities but he asked them politely to be quiet. I could sense a great keenness in the air. Everyone was sympathetic, and people were muttering things like, "Poor little puppy. Hope he doesn't die." But I was concentrating now and, in a while, I forgot all other distractions.

We went down the road, round a sheltered bus-stop, into an alcove by a tobacco-shop and here I sniffed and stopped.

Woof said, "The man hid here for some seconds. He must have waited to see if I was following."

The crowd nodded and murmured and expressed some awe at this bit of detective work. Then I continued.

The trail led back parallel to the way we had come but on the opposite kerb. By now the crowd behind us had swelled and there was a great deal of anger expressed against the killer.

We were now at the entrance to a residential building. Here the crowd stopped.

A few feet from the main entrance was a set of steps. It led to a little verandah or balcony and at the back of it was a door. The scent was very strong here. I pushed at the door with a paw. It was not locked. It opened. I led Woof into a drawing room.

A woman's voice called, "Who's that?"

Woof said, "I'm sorry to barge in like this but is there anyone else here?"

She came out of the kitchen with a knife and a potato in her hand. She was polite and asked Woof to sit down. He said, "No thank you. I'm looking for someone who was by the dhobi's shack a while ago."

"Why?" she asked with some consternation.

"He almost killed my dog with a stone."

"Oh." She seemed to go pale and the knife in her hand shook. Then she recovered and said, "But how do you know he came here?"

"The dog brought me here," Woof said.

"The dog?" the woman said.

"Yes, he's a tracker. And he'll never forget the man who hurt him, unless I introduce the man to him as a friend. It's for the man's own safety that I'm here."

That was a lot of hoosh. I mean, I was not ever going to attack a man uncommanded but Woof was being clever. He suspected the woman was shielding someone and he wanted to play on her worry and get her to bring out the culprit. You see that's how it is working as a detective dog. A police dog who is in the police force could go straight into a kitchen or bedroom and arrest a man. Not so a detective dog. I had to wait for the culprit to be brought out into the drawing-room.

The woman was afraid. She made an excuse. She said, "It may have been my son. He was out all evening and came back just now but he's gone out again."

Now that was a lie. He was somewhere inside. I growled. But Woof gave me the hand signal—a knotted fist—to keep quiet and I did.

"Very well, then," Woof said. "We'll go home. But tell him that I know and the dog knows. And the dog may catch him one day, unless he comes to me and apologizes."

"I'll tell him," she said, and came to the door with us. Then she saw the large crowd outside and exclaimed, "What's this?"

"Your son has been killing dogs for no reason," Woof said, "and these people are angry about it."

"He . . . he's afraid of dogs," she stammered.

"That's not true," said a teenager from the crowd. "I know your son, Aunty. He's not afraid of dogs. If he was, he wouldn't dare go near them to throw a stone. He hates them."

"But why?" Woof asked.

"Because," said the teenager, "all through his childhood he

wanted a puppy and he was not allowed to have one."

The crowd laughed at that but Woof nodded and said, "There may be some truth in it." Then he turned to the lady and said, "I'd like to have a word with you privately if I may."

She nodded and went back into the drawing-room. Woof asked me to sit outside the door. I did, and a number of people came up from the crowd and petted me.

Woof was in the drawing-room for just a few minutes. When he came out he had a piece of paper in his hand. He put it in his pocket and we went home, but the crowd remained hanging about the culprit's house, commenting on how I had tracked him down.

At home, Woof gave me some dog biscuits soaked in broth as a reward for a job well done and he sat down with a cup of hot coffee to discuss with Wuff the strange case of the killer.

It must have been around midnight that I heard the peculiar squeak of the killer's crepe-soled shoes outside the door. I jumped up with a little bark. I couldn't help the bark; this was an emergency. Woof was beside me in a trice.

Just then the doorbell rang. A number of young boys and others had accompanied the killer to our door. One of them said, "We have brought him to you to apologize."

Woof was quite overcome. "Thank you," he said. He listened as the killer said he was sorry and began to cry. He was a nineteen-year-old boy.

Woof then brought me out and let me sniff at him. I immediately caught his right hand to indicate that he was the killer.

Woof reassured me that the case was now closed. I sat down and watched, on the alert and wondering what Woof would do with the culprit.

"I could hand you over to the police," Woof said and the boy trembled, "but I'll content myself with making sure that you go to the other dog-owners and apologize. They will probably ask the Society for the Prevention of Cruelty to Animals to deal with you. But as for your attack on my dog, Ranjha, I have what I think is a very appropriate punishment for you. This."

He took out of his pocket the piece of paper and said, "It's a note written by your mother. It's a promise that within the week she will get you a pup of your choice."

The boy was startled by that. For a while a tremendous struggle seemed to be going on within him. He clenched and unclenched his hands, he bit his lower lip and his entire body seemed to shake with sobs. Tears trickled down his cheeks. He clasped Woof's hand in both his.

"Oh, thank you, thank you, sir," he said.

"Not at all," said Woof. "You don't realise what a punishment it will be to you. With every passing day you will love your puppy more and more; at the same time you will remember, with increasing sadness, how once you killed dogs."

And that is what happened. We used to see the boy after that, walking about happily with his Cocker Spaniel pup. Then he would notice us and he would look down, ashamed, and the tears would gather in his eyes.

We never asked him what punishment he was given by the other people whose pets he had killed, or what compensations were demanded of him. Perhaps he had to face charges in court. Perhaps his family had to pay heavy fines on his behalf. It was enough for us to know that his attitude to other animals had been changed forever by his love for a little Cocker Spaniel pup.

4

The Case of the Missing Labrador

I t still surprises me that both my earliest cases were concerned with dogs. But that is how it was.

A few days after we had solved the mystery of the sudden killer we were whirled into the case of the missing Labrador.

That evening, as it grew dark, we turned off the racecourse after our walk. The racecourse has a number of gates and at each gate there are usually a couple of *chowkidars* or watchmen, Ram Prasad, the *chowkidar* at the nearest gate, was a friendly sort. So we stopped by the gate to have a chat with him. Woof offered him a cigarette and they stood about smoking and discussing the weather. It was a pleasant evening and everything seemed calm as usual.

Then suddenly there was a commotion at a farther gate. Ram Prasad stubbed out his cigarette and, excusing himself, went forward to investigate. A two-tone limousine roared up with its horn blaring. Ram Prasad held up his hand to stop the car but it swung on to the tracks almost knocking the *chowkidar* over. He began shouting and running after the car but the tail-lights could be seen speeding away round the innermost track. The horn was still blaring and the driver could be heard yelling something.

Meanwhile, two other *chowkidars* had now joined Ram Prasad and they all began gesticulating and quickly put up a barricade of horse-jumps. The car came round with its headlights on full. For a moment it seemed as though it would go smashing through the barricade. Then it stopped.

There was a heated exchange between the *chowkidars* and the uniformed chauffeur in the limousine. Then the shouting subsided into expressions of sympathy.

Woof looked at me and shrugged and we started moving away to the place where our car was parked.

Just then Ram Prasad came up, shouting, "Sahib! Sahib!"

Woof and I stopped.

Ram Prasad said, "The big car belongs to Sir G.D., the famous racehorse owner. He has a stable of fifteen horses."

"Well?" Woof said with a slight edge in his voice. He is no respecter of wealth and position. He treats everyone equally and simply as fellow-animals.

"Well," said Ram Prasad, "his son has a couple of white Labradors and one of them has been stolen or lost. Ganpat Shinde, the chauffeur, was asked to take them for a walk but he didn't. Instead he sat down to have a cup of tea with a friend and when he came back one of the dogs was missing from the car. Shinde fears he's going to lose his job for this. Poor man, how could he know that someone would want to steal a white Labrador?"

"It's unlikely that such a big dog would be stolen," Woof said, "but it's possible. There are dognappers about."

"He was a champion show dog," Ram Prasad said. "You must have heard of him, the famous Werner von Bremen. He cost as much as a racehorse. They were going to breed more champions from him. Poor Shinde, such a good chauffeur with a such a good job! Now he'll be out on the street for this."

Another *chowkidar* had come up by now. He said, "The dog was called White Werner by everyone. Like God's own dream he was when he stood and posed, leaning forward, with his hind legs stretching taut as a bow behind him. Surely you must have heard of him."

"I don't care much for dog shows and show dogs," Woof said turning away. "I prefer dogs that work."

"But, Sahib, you must help Shinde, the poor chauffeur."

Woof stopped. "Certainly. But how?"

"Why, Sahib," said Ram Prasad, "you have a detective dog. Surely he can find out who stole Werner."

Woof considered the matter for a while. Then he looked at the limousine with its headlights on and the engine still running and the chauffeur standing outside by the barricade, peering anxiously at us. Woof looked at his watch. Some guests were coming to dinner. We would be late. Wuff would worry. But this was an emergency.

"All right," Woof said. "There's no harm in trying. It'll also be good practice for Ranjha."

Ram Prasad said, "Thank you, sahib. I knew you would agree. I told Shinde you would."

We went up to the chauffeur. He took off his cap and twisted it in his hands. There were tears in his eyes and his face was creased with worry.

"Werner wouldn't jump out of the car normally, sir," he said. "He's never done such a thing before. I've looked for him everywhere. He would at least respond to my shouts, if not to the car horn. But there's no sign of him."

"How long have you been searching now?"

"Three hours, sir."

"Three hours!"

"Yes, sir." The chauffeur nodded hopelessly. "I've searched and shouted. I've driven all the way home three times. The servants at the house told me he hasn't shown up. The *chowkidar* here say they haven't see him."

"Who's that?" Woof asked pointing to a white Labrador bitch sitting dolefully in the back of the Plymouth.

"That's Renate, sir. Werner's mate. We've been trying to bring them together, sir, but Werner can't stand her somehow. It's two years now, sir, and she's not had any puppies. Werner's pups could fetch a lot of money, sir."

"Hm." Woof petted Renate but she hung her head down sadly. "Poor thing. She seems terribly depressed."

"She's always been like that, sir, ever since we got her as a companion for Werner."

"Well," said Woof in a brisker tone and I knew we were about to begin working, "take me to the exact spot from where he was lost."

"If you will come with me, sir—" The chauffeur opened the door of the limousine but Woof waved him into the driving seat.

"We'll follow in our car," he said.

We went to our car and got in. The *chowkidars* removed the barricades and the Plymouth careered away.

"He drives like a madman and shouts like a sergeant-major," Woof muttered. "No wonder the dog doesn't respond to his calling—that is, if the dog is around."

We pulled up behind the Plymouth as it slowed to a stop half a mile away. We were in front of a slum consisting of hundreds of ramshackle dwellings.

The chauffeur came running up to us as we got out.

"I was in there, sir," he said pointing to the nearest hut, "having a cup of tea with a friend. The car was parked exactly where it is and, in the ten minutes that I was away, the dog was gone."

Woof took out the length of webbing from the boot and tried on my improvised harness—I was still too small for a proper one.

"Now then," Woof said, "it'll be of great help if you can give me something belonging to Werner the white Labrador. Perhaps you have a cloth or a cushion or a rug on which he normally sat."

The chauffeur looked dismayed. "Oh, sir, for that I'd have to go back to the house."

Again Woof looked at his watch. It was half past eight and he was thinking of his guests awaiting him at home.

Then the chauffeur had an idea. "Would Werner's collar do, sir? We take it off whenever we can. It spoils his coat. The collar's in the car."

"Good," Woof said. "Let me have it. Be sure to hold it by the buckle, otherwise you'll get your scent on it."

I took one sniff of the collar and began investigation. Werner's scent was everywhere. He had wandered around all over the place. His trail was a series of interlocking doodles.

A small group of curious people had naturally gathered by now and watched me. But soon their interest lessened. I went on and on, circling and criss-crossing the area. A number of them laughed, shrugged their shoulders and went off about their own business. Finally, the chauffeur said, "This dog's just fooling around. It's a waste of time."

He began to walk about, calling to Werner. After a few minutes of this, he climbed into the limousine again and was about to drive off to repeat his earlier desperate honking and shouting, when Woof said, "Just a minute, Ganpat Shinde."

"Yes, sir?"

"Why did you lie?"

"About what, sir?"

"You said you were gone from the car just ten minutes, but Ranjha has been following Werner's meandering footsteps for the last half hour. That means you were inside the hut for at least that length of time."

The chauffeur went red in the face and bit his lip.

"Well, sir," he said, "to tell you the truth I was inside more than an hour—"

"What were you doing all that time?"

"I didn't like to say that at first, sir, because it might have got back to my master that I wasted so much time here and neglected the dogs."

"What were you doing inside?" Woof repeated sternly.

"I . . . I, sir . . . I have a friend who lives here with her family, a maidservant who I propose to marry when I can afford it and—"

"I see," said Woof with a laugh. "So you were courting. And were the dogs really in the car or were they loose?"

"Oh no, sir. They were in the car. I daren't let them wander around, especially here. In fact I had the glasses of the windows up so that they couldn't jump out. You see, sir, there are other dogs about and my master would be most upset if Werner and Renate mixed with them."

"What do you mean when you say you wouldn't let them wander around, especially here?"

"Just what I said, sir. There are a lot of strays here and—"

He was distracted by the appearance of a good-looking young woman who draped herself about the doorway of the hut. She stared at him with a mixture of insolence and triumph. He began to splutter and fume.

"It's all your fault!" he cried. "I know it's all your doing!"

She gave a short contemptuous laugh, shrugged and went indoors. He was furious. Taking off his cap he seemed undecided whether to fling it after her or trample it underfoot. Then he climbed into the front seat of the limousine and started up.

Woof shouted, "Hey!"

He said, "She let the dog out! I know she slipped out and did that. She wants to get her own back because I couldn't get her a pup of Werner's." And with that he zoomed away, howling and calling out, "Werner! Werner!"

Woof bent down and patted me. "Well," he said, "we might as well try a little more. It's too late to welcome my guests for dinner and it's too late to turn back. I know we're on the trail. Let's keep on it."

He gave me another sniff of Werner's collar and the commands, "Scent. Track. Catch."

If Woof says "Catch", I know I'm to track a living being. If he says "Fetch", I know I'm to collect evidence. So I set off to catch Werner. I had tracked men before but never a dog. I knew Woof was wondering whether I would hesitate to track another dog.

In ten minutes the trail led towards the racecourse. The chauffeur had been right in his assumption that Werner would head that way. It was the only safe hiding place in this part of the teeming city. But the stands and paddocks, the cafeteria, the stables and grounds cover an area of about six square miles. Werner could be hiding anywhere.

As I followed Werner's scent across the road and through the outer gates, I began to be troubled by a creepy sensation in my nostrils. I analysed it quickly. Yes, along with Werner's scent there were two others, and all of them had moved together towards the racecourse.

It was pitch dark now. We were on the grounds of what is called the First Enclosure. This is a huge building with tiers of benches for racegoers. Then we crossed the racetrack with its smell of sawdust and horse dung and we were in the high grass of the central meadow. I knew that Woof was worrying—he was stepping high and carefully. At this time, snakes come out and many of them are deadly poisonous. I was strong on the scent now. We went on.

The trio had turned again and this time they had moved towards the Third Enclosure. This area is fenced like the others but it is always kept locked. Woof tugged at my harness once, as though to say, "Surely, Ranjha, you are wrong. There's no way of getting into that."

The chauffeur and *chowkidars*, too, had ignored this part. We could hear the car and see its headlights two miles away across the flat ground. I pulled forward and came to a gap in the hedge and a missing stake in the fence. Woof hesitated. He seemed uncertain and I gave a little growl.

Woof held me in and turning towards the distant car he shouted, "Shinde! Shinde! Werner is here!" But of course the car was too far away.

A *chowkidar* came running. Woof sent him off for the chauffeur. We waited. Shinde obviously needed to be persuaded. He took a long time. When he finally joined us, Woof said, "Werner may bite if he is approached by a stranger. He may be off his head; who knows? Anyway, he's in there. Go and get him."

Shinde said, "But how do I get in?"

"Like this," Woof said in exasperation and we all crawled in through the hedge and the fence.

I put my nose to the ground and raced forward. Suddenly there he was at the end of the enclosure, dimly visible, white in the night like a ghost. Beside him were two other shapes.

"Damn it!" Shinde said. "He ran off with those bitches."

The chauffeur rushed forward. The trio separated. Werner dodged and barked and evaded Shinde. A dog is so much faster than a man that it's useless to try and chase him. You have either to cajole him or corner him.

"Wait!" Woof said to Shinde. The chauffeur stopped. "You'll never catch him if he is determined to elude you. Let's ask Ranjha to help."

"Ranjha?" the chauffeur said incredulously.

Woof released me from the harness with the command, "Arrest!"

Werner was startled to see a young pup coming towards him. He couldn't believe that a pup would do anything other than fool around. I must confess I was frightened. Werner was even bigger than Tughlak, and here I was having the audacity to challenge him. But the element of surprise was in my favour. Werner darted to the side—too late. I was already there, snarling. I was now close enough to see him clearly. He blinked and growled, "What the hell are you doing, puppy?"

"Arresting you, sir," I said.

"For what?" he snapped. "For falling in love with two beautiful strays? Is falling in love a crime?"

"I sympathize, sir," I said, "but I have my orders."

"Orders, *graah*!" he growled. "Get out of my way. For two years I've been tied to that wet rag, Renate. Now I've met these delightful gypsies of the street, I'm not going back."

"I'm sorry, sir," I said and I meant it. I was sorry for him.

Fortunately I didn't need to say any more. Seeing us snarling at each other, Woof had quickly improvised a lasso from the harness and now he swung it over Werner. Werner was led back to the car.

However, I'm glad to report that the case had a happy ending. As we crawled out of the Third Enclosure, we were met by a portly gentleman in a suit.

"I'm V.K.," he said. "Sir G.D.'s son and Werner's owner."

The family seemed to prefer talking in initials. I wouldn't have been surprised if he addressed his dog Werner as W.V.B.

V.K. shook hands with Woof. The chauffeur had already been profuse in his thanks. Now V.K. said, "So sorry you were troubled like this. I knew something had happened when the dogs weren't back by eight o'clock. It's ten now and I thought I just had to come and see. The *chowkidars* had told me all about you and your dog—but, my God, what a little pup he is! I expected a huge animal."

Woof laughed and said, "He'll grow."

"I really don't know how to thank you. Werner is quite clever. He would never have been found without your help. Isn't there something I can do by way of compensating for the time you've wasted?"

"No, no," said Woof. "It's good practice for Ranjha and a good story to take home to my guests. They must have had their dinner by now if—" Woof chuckled and continued—"if the old stove hasn't broken down again. But yes, there are a few things you can do for Shinde and Werner and Renate, if you'll permit me to make a few suggestions."

"Certainly, certainly," V.K. said.

"The first thing, V.K.," Woof said stopping and turning to face him, "is to marry Shinde, the chauffeur, to his girl-friend. He needs a little financial assistance."

"No problem in that. No problem at all," V.K. nodded.

"Once married, Shinde will not be tempted to spend his

evenings there. And, of course, after this he'll be far more conscientious. Next, I suggest you find another companion for Renate—"

"Well," V.K. interrupted, "I had been considering that. You see, I think she's in love with her previous kennel-mate. And her lovesick attitude has been telling on Werner. He has become a shadow of himself but you wouldn't think that to look at him at this moment. I've never known him so sparky!"

Woof chuckled and said, "That's because he was running about with two bitches just now."

"Oh no!"

"But there's no harm in that. It'll help you to keep him cheerful."

"Of course, of course," V.K. muttered distractedly, and began walking on. Then he stopped again. "But strays are so prone to carry infection. They might give him rabies or distemper or something."

" I was coming to that. I suggest you have them vaccinated."

"What? The strays?"

"Yes, why not? I think they belong to Shinde's lady-friend. She'll be grateful and, of course, her pets will have more Werner puppies than she asked for."

"I don't know. I don't know," V.K. muttered. "Of course I could still breed from him the way I want to."

"Think about it," Woof said, and with that we returned to our car and came home.

The next evening I discovered I was the hero of the race-course. Word had spread about the solving of the Werner case and many of the humans there wanted to see me. V.K. also came, this time in another car, and he came bearing gifts as a reward— a box of chocolates for Woof, a bag of biscuits for me and best of all an expensive new gas-cooker to take home to Wuff. It more than made up for the dinner we had missed the night before.

"So," said Tughlak with a rather pig-like grunt, "you're now a little hero around here. I tell you it's getting difficult to walk about with you. Everyone turns to look."

"It's not my fault," I said apologetically.

"I suppose not," Tughlak agreed. "But let me warn you, boy, any little bit of showing off from you and I'll avoid your company like the plague. I'll drop you like a hot brick. It disturbs my peace of mind to have everyone staring at us like that. So one little bit of flap-de-doodle showing off and I'll strike you off my social list. At the moment, I accept that it's not your fault."

"Thank you," I said and took care to walk a paw's width behind him.

But I could see that he was not only pleased but proud to be with me.

5

A Vet Day in My Life

One effect of being trained as a detective dog was that every part of me began to function well separately and at the same time was in excellent co-ordination with the other parts. I felt as though I were a friendly army on the move. Let me explain.

My ears were like radar. My nose was like a spy system. My eyes were like a patrol of advance scouts. My legs were, of course, the transport division. And the rest of me moved forward, prepared for whatever lay ahead. All that I sensed or felt was transmitted quickly to my brain, the headquarters, where it was analysed, sifted and collated. Important information was then put into a special code and the message flashed to the general, my master, who would then signal back his orders.

Talking of signals, communication between Woof and me had come to such a point that he needed only to give me a specific hand signal without any verbal command and I could understand what he expected of me.

One finger held before me meant that I should sit. An open palm held horizontal meant that I should lie down. The open palm held sideways and moved stiffly to one side meant that I should stand. The open palm moved upwards meant that I should speak—it was often useful, this deliberate barking, for it helped to give others a warning. A closed fist meant that I should keep quiet. An open palm held vertical meant that I should stay where I was. A forward sweep of the arm meant that I should go ahead.

A signal to the left or the right indicated which way I should move, and the palm held inwards and brought back towards the face recalled me from an advance position. A hand held close to the side with the fingers patting the thigh meant that I should go to heel. Then, of course, there was the obvious signal for "no"—a finger wagged from side to side. These were only a few of the words in our growing vocabulary. In the next three months, the total was to exceed fifty-five commands.

What I started out to say when I talked of being a friendly army on the move is that I found myself less afraid, less inclined to give in to indefinable fears. Woof took me to all sorts of places—noisy factories and crowded bazaars, jungles full of wild animals and abandoned houses as still as the grave. I learnt to go up and down creaking staircases. I learnt to climb shaky ladders, though in the beginning Woof had to hold them steady from below. I learnt to stand solitary and still as a statue on a great height and await the command before making my way down. I learnt to overcome my fear.

But one fear I had some difficulty in coping with was fear of the Vet.

He was a bald man with strange powers like a magician. He jabbed dogs with long hypodermic needles and made their masters hold them down as they lay shivering on a brass-topped table that had a little drain down the centre. He had an assistant, too, who chewed *pan* and spat out of the window of this first-floor dispensary in a crowded locality of Bombay. The assistant never spoke; he only cleared his throat and pinned the dog's hindlegs down. The Vet would then adjust his spectacles, load

the barrel of the injector and, having swabbed the dog's stomach with something cold and chilling, he would stab the dog with the long needle, chatting casually all the while.

The first time I went to the Vet I was so young and small I didn't know what was happening. That was for the first dose of puppy vaccine—anti-rabies and distemper. But the second time that I went an incident occurred that had a long-lasting effect on me.

I had come up the stairs quietly enough. And I walked into the office and lay down beside my master's chair and watched all the Pekes and Poms and Poodles getting restless waiting and being petted or held in on leashes. It was a hot day and I let my tongue hang out but I breathed easy as I surveyed all these little breeds. Some of them were already whimpering and begging for mercy. I remember feeling quite brave. Perhaps I was being a little arrogant as well. After all, I was obviously the most highly educated dog among them and I was bigger and better-groomed with my shiny black and tan coat and my eyes sparkling with confidence and my altogether handsome looks—although one of my ears still flopped and my tail seemed too long. But I was strong.

The old ladies or servants who accompanied the other pets were as nervous as their charges. My master was calm. I looked up at him and I felt a tingle of pride. I looked about me and felt on top of the world.

In the adjoining room, around the brass-topped table, were other people waiting with their dogs. There were Terriers, Dobermans, Dachshunds, Dalmatians, Retrievers and there were some of indeterminate pedigree. A Spaniel was on the table and the Vet was pressing some pills into its mouth. After each pill, the Spaniel would howl something quite obscene. It's a good thing the Vet didn't understand him.

In our room, a Scottie had climbed into the Vet's swivel chair and was examining the papers and bills on the desk. His mistress was absorbed in the drama of the reluctant Spaniel and didn't realise that the Scottie was free.

"Hoots, mon," the Scottie growled. "What a madhouse! And they make you pay for it, too!"

He had just picked up a wad of bills when his mistress saw him. She clapped her hands sharply and called him. But the Scottie took the wad of bills in his mouth and, leaping off the chair, he ran about among the dogs. The smaller ones leaped into their mistresses' laps or scuttled out of the way. Some barked, others wagged their tails and wanted to join in the game. The Scottie's mistress was trying to reach him under chairs and around people and between dogs. I sat up and looked at Woof but he was laughing; we were not to interfere.

Just then a Great Dane came in. He was *huge*, as huge as a young mule. Scottie was darting for the door when he was confronted by this mammoth creature. He let out a little yip and shrank in terror. But he needn't have worried—the Great Dane was friendly and also he was pre-occupied; he had problems of his own. With a mournful look, the Great Dane watched as the Scottie's mistress collected him, then he padded sadly into the room dragging a beautiful young sari-clad lady behind him. She had stopped to talk to someone on the landing of the stairs but the Great Dane was so absorbed in his own thoughts that he quite forgot she was attached to him by a leash. He chose a spot and sat down. The lady whom he had brought along was obviously someone very special, for the Vet's assistant stepped in quickly, bowed, smiled and placed a chair for her by her pet.

In a few seconds, the Great Dane was inclined to stand up and stretch. When he did that he took up half the room; and then he was not inclined to sit down. I have forgotten now what his exact name was but I think she called him something quite unsuitable like Fido. Fido refused to sit. The lady looked about her helplessly and prettily. The assistant happened to notice and again came tripping in. She shrugged and said, "This room is too small."

He shrugged in reply and gave a little laugh of apology.

Woof was chuckling. The assistant looked at him and said in a whisper of annoyance, "She lives in a great mansion in acres of garden. She's not used to this."

When the assistant had gone in again, the lady sighed, "Oh, dear, what a stupid mutt my Fido is!" She turned to everyone in the room and said, "We've had him trained by a professional but he just won't listen to me. He's one of the dumbest beasts I've ever seen."

Woof laughed and said, "I think he's been trained but you haven't been."

She looked at him sharply but saw that he had said it good-humouredly.

"What am I to do?" She sighed charmingly.

"I suggest," Woof said, "that you spend a little more time— just ten minutes a day—training him yourself. Then you will know what to do. Right now, for instance, you have him on a choke-chain—"

"But it doesn't help!" she wailed. "He's so strong that he just ignores it."

Woof nodded and continued, "If you were to pull up on the collar and press down on his back over his hindlegs, he would learn to sit in five minutes."

"All right," she said and, giving Fido the command, she tried it. He sat down at once.

"Marvellous!" she cried. But now that she had got her dog to obey once, she was not concerned to go on with the topic of dog-training. She was, as they say, scatterbrained. She preferred social small talk.

Woof tried to bring her back to the subject of her dog. She said gaily, "Oh he's just a pup, a silly little pup!"

"A pup?" Woof said.

"Yes," she nodded. "He's only eight months."

"Ranjha, here, is eight months, too," Woof said. "But what a massive animal your Fido is! At eight months he's big enough to sit on a man and keep him down."

"Yes," she laughed, "and the terrible thing is he still thinks he's a lap dog, a regular little mama's darling."

Fido was looking about him with a mixture of worry and hopelessness and now stood up again. But his mistress was talking brightly of other things. Fido felt in need of a bit of attention. He tried to bring his head under her waving, gesticulating hands and thus receive at least a passing caress but she ignored him. Then suddenly she noticed that he was standing again. She interrupted herself and said, "Fido, sit down!"

Fido was not such a dumb mutt as she had supposed. He had learnt the meaning of the command at the very first go. But now he varied its application to suit himself. With a slight sideways movement, he lowered himself slowly.

"Not in my lap, you fool!" she cried.

But it was too late. He had sat down in her lap, on her lap and all over her. The chair under her collapsed. Fido looked around him sadly, absorbed in his own thoughts, heedless of the fact that his mistress was pinned under him. She heaved at him, called to him, but he was oblivious of everything except his own worry. What that was we discovered in a moment.

The Vet appeared at the door. A pair of forceps and a pair of tongs fell clattering from his hands. "What's going on?" he cried.

The appearance of the Vet had a terrifying effect on Fido. He tried to squeeze himself smaller and turn invisible. He wanted his mistress to protect him from this egg-headed ogre. But the Vet was a wizard with more charms in his cupboard and spells in his books than Fido would ever know. He fumbled about in a drawer of the desk and brought out a packet of biscuits. He held one out and called, "Fido!"

Fido forgot his fear and leaped forward, clamping his jaws round the falling biscuit. His mistress was free.

The Vet ushered us in and said to the lady, "If Your Highness will please wait a few minutes more . . ."

"Of course," she smiled, brushing herself and rearranging her sari.

But Fido had put the fear of the Vet into me.

I allowed myself to be lifted on to the high brass-topped table but the moment I saw the needle, the syringe and the gleam in the Vet's eyes, I began to try to jump off. Woof, my best friend, my master, held me down. The assistant had my legs. The Vet moved in close. I squirmed and snarled and turned my head to snap at him. But then he took out a scarf and tied a sort of muzzle over my mouth. I lay back whimpering and helpless and I was given my second shot of anti-rabies vaccine. It wasn't too unpleasant and I was well enough in a second to jump down and wag my tail and be petted, even by the Vet. It was just that Fido had communicated his fear to me. After all, who can say that a Great Dane is not strong? I had reasoned that if a Great Dane could go into a funk, there must be enough in it to make an Alsatian afraid.

But, of course, Great Danes can be wrong. A few more visits to the Vet and I realised that he used all his wizardry to cure me if I was ill and to heal my wounds if I was injured. As a pup, I was bitten once or twice by bad-tempered and badly-trained dogs. It was the Vet who dressed my wounds and reassured Woof. Once he saved my life. I would have bled to death from a gash deep inside one of my nostrils—I had accidentally spiked myself on the thin rod-like handle of the hood on the baby's pram; it was the Vet who gave me an injection that stopped the bleeding. He was most concerned that this injury should heal completely for otherwise it would have meant the end of my career as a tracker dog. Again, it was the Vet who advised on the amount of food I should be given. I was having two meals a day now consisting of boiled meat, vegetables and left-over scraps. Of course, I could have eaten the meat raw but the Vet insisted it should be boiled so that there was no danger of worms or germs in it.

Only day the Vet offered me a biscuit just as he had done with the Great Dane. I did not move towards it. I stayed sitting where I was and ignored it. The Vet was amazed.

"What's the matter with him?" he asked.

Woof said casually, "Oh, he's all right. It's just that he's been trained not to eat anything without a command from me."

"Very good!" the Vet exclaimed. "That's one way of stopping him from eating rubbish off the street."

"Yes," Woof agreed, and added, "It's also one way of ensuring that the criminals he goes after can't poison him."

The Vet gave an indulgent laugh and said, "Yes, yes, of course." But from that day on he began to take a keen interest in how I was being trained. Most of all he was pleased that he, too, was helping to keep me fit and healthy for the cases that lay ahead. Perhaps he was as surprised as Woof and I at the number of cases on which I eventually worked. All I know is that from the moment I solved my first major case, he began to hang photographs of me in his dispensary.

6

The Case of the Caddie's Ring

My first major case took place in Mahabaleshwar. It came to be known as the Case of the Caddie's Ring.

Abdul Rahman was a fine old caddie and a more unique person than his name conveys, for Abdul Rahman is a very common name in India and indeed in all the East. What was obviously unusual about him at first sight was that he wore a large red fez. Now the fashion of wearing a fez has faded in most Eastern countries but Abdul Rahman wore it with the same quaint individuality that marks out a man who still affects a solar topee.

Abdul Rahman was a dark, polite, toothless man who somehow always managed to have a grizzled face. The stubble on his chin was white, of course, and it seemed as if he never shaved, though a bit of grizzly stubble can hardly be called a beard. He dressed in baggy clothes, not by choice but by necessity. They were usually old coats and trousers given to him as parting gifts by golfers who had stayed in the Mahabaleshwar Club.

It was outside this sedate institution that he could be seen most often, that is when he wasn't out on the links teaching someone to play or behaving generally like the best caddie this side of Bombay.

The family and I saw him almost every day, and we would often stop to talk. He was a little afraid of me but that was because he sometimes watched me at my training exercises and regarded me with a mixture of respect and awe. He didn't realise how much I liked him. He was kind and good and gentle and he was courteous in all his conversations with Woof.

Being a detective dog, it had become second nature to me now to observe and sniff as many people as I could. Abdul Rahman smelt of *beedis*—of which he smoked a vast number—and slightly damp warm clothes, with a touch of coconut hair oil, a dash of the scent of leather from the handles of golf clubs, with a pinch of garlic and the faintest aroma of spiced meat and salted cucumber. There was more to the smell of Abdul Rahman but suffice it to say that I could identify him with my eyes shut from among the numerous other caddies who stood around by the road waiting for the tourist or visitor who might wish to play.

But, as I said, even at first sight, he stood out. And that is probably why he made a little more money than the others and was able, by scrimping and saving, to put by five hundred rupees for the marriage of his only daughter. He was a trusting, talkative man and as the wedding day approached everyone knew that he went about with all his savings in the pocket of his baggy coat.

Then one afternoon he was assaulted and robbed and left for dead on the golf course.

Most people on holiday take a little nap after lunch. The sun is hottest at that time and only a sports fanatic would think of golfing at that hour. So it was that afternoon, and Abdul Rahman, being free, had taken the opportunity of going down to the links, by the fifth hole, near the old cemetery, to find a ball that had been lost. The tee is up on a wooded hillock and the cemetery sprawls in the cleaning below along the nearer edge of the green.

I knew this place well, as indeed I knew the entire golf course, for I had often been sent out by Woof to help old Abdul Rahman and his *agewallahs*. *Agewallahs* mean literally "forward men" and perhaps the term is unique to Mahabaleshwar for it signifies the three or four men who stand to the fore watching where the ball has gone. The golf course is an adventurous one with all sorts of obstacles and difficult terrain. Two or three balls are lost on each round. And, of course, whoever finds them later stands to gain. So the caddies and the *agewallahs* scrounge the terrain each afternoon for the balls that were declared lost in the morning. And that is what Abdul Rahman was about that afternoon.

He was thrashing the undergrowth with a putter hoping the ball would pop out, when someone with a bandage wrapped all over his face and only a slit left open for his eyes, stepped from behind a tree and swung at Abdul Rahman with a stick.

The old man was quick enough to duck but he was so shocked by the sight of the masked face that he failed to avoid the second blow. It struck the centre of his fez. That probably softened the blow but it was enough to knock him unconscious. When he revived, he found himself bleeding from a gash in the head. His money was gone and along with it his watch, his hardly-usable pen and his ring. The ring was not precious and it was not much of an ornament, either. He had bought it in place of his wedding ring which he had sold many years before. This cheap ring which he had now taken to wearing was like hundreds of others sold in the bazaar; and it had a red stone that could have passed for a ruby. Abdul Rahman's watch, too, had been an inexpensive one that hardly ever kept correct time. He felt nothing for the loss of these things but the loss of the money was a disaster. He almost died of heart failure as the thought came to him that his daughter's marriage might not now take place. Most of the money was to have been her dowry. The tailor from Bombay who was the groom had sent his uncle to say that he would not be satisfied with anything less than three hundred rupees. The rest of the money would have gone in the celebrations and a big

meal for the relatives. By other people's standards it may not have been a large amount but to Abdul Rahman it was a fortune.

Now he cried and bled and struggled painfully up the hillside.

It was his elder son, Mohammed, who came to the house and informed Woof. Abdul Rahman had asked for help. He had some sort of faith in me. He wanted me to be brought there to track the attacker.

You must not think that I am some sort of a genius among dogs and that I understood at once all that had happened. Oh no, I had to piece the whole thing together, bit by bit, and what I have related already I came to know only gradually by reconstruction from all that I heard and saw and smelt. All what was immediately clear to me was that Mohammed had arrived and spoken to my master and I was being put in the harness. Now, for the first time, I was going into the proper tracking harness. At last I was big enough for it. I knew already, though, that straps going loosely round my belly and neck meant that I was about to track. It excited me. I was rested and fresh. I was ready. I was eager.

When we arrived at the spot, I knew it was Abdul Rahman's blood I smelt. He had been taken to the doctor, but I immediately understood that Abdul Rahman had been struck. As I sniffed around, I knew he had been struck with the stick, the stick that lay there on the ground.

"Have you informed the police yet?" Woof asked.

Mohammed said, "My father would rather not till we are sure who the culprit is. You see, he suspects a distant cousin of his, a man called Suleiman who sells strawberries. Suleiman wanted to marry his own daughter to the tailor from Bombay. My father suspects that Suleiman got someone to do this so that the wedding of my sister would be called off."

"But that's no reason not to go to the police. He can't shield a criminal simply because he is a cousin."

"That's not it, sahib. You see, if my father goes to the police he will have to state his suspicions. Then they will question my uncle and if, after all that, my uncle turns out to be innocent, it will leave a terrible rift in the family. My father doesn't wish to go to the police till he is sure it isn't his cousin. It would be a public scandal, you see. That's why I haven't been allowed to tell anyone else about this yet. My brothers would go and beat up my uncle and, after all, he's an old man, too. We are only wanting to know if the trail of the attacker leads to my uncle's hut and farm. If that is so, then we know that the attacker went back to him to report."

"All right," Woof said. "Let's go."

Then he had a second thought. He said, "But others must have seen your father bleeding and hurt."

"Yes," said Mohammed, "but he told them he fell down the hillside and gashed his head on a gravestone."

Woof said, "All right," again and holding my nose to the stick he said, "Ranjha, scent, track, catch!"

The smell on the stick was clear. If I subtracted the smell of the wood itself and the sugary sap in it, for this part of the branch had obviously been hacked recently from a tree, I arrived at the undiluted smell of the man who had wielded it. The man's smell was quite intricate and carried within it the essence of aniseed, beetlenut, lime, tobacco, toddy, perspiration, old clothes, pickled mango, stale *chappatis*, onions and, most dominant of all, the odour of the fleece of sheep. The trail was as forceful as a mountain stream; it went straight down the hill in a panic. The man must have slithered down, holding on to the trunks of trees, grasping at branches, stumbling on immovable rocks. On the ground, his scent was compounded with that of the odour on his footwear and the old hide of which it was made. He was obviously wearing a common type of lace-less shoes known as *mojris*.

All the way down the hillock the trail held good, for the scent was caught in the windless woods and held by the leaves and shrubbery. On the green, too, the trail remained clear. I had only to subtract the smell of the different types of grass. Sometimes I would pause and take a second sniff at one spot, just to be sure, and then I would become aware again of Woof's gentle encouragement and his holding on to the long leash, and Mohammed standing keenly behind him. But much of the time I was absorbed in my own calculations.

Two miles later we were crossing a cart-track of rubble when I went straight ahead and almost lost the trail. I doubled back a few yards and examined the ground air again. Ah, he took the left fork; he had decided to stick to the rubble road. He must have been running, for though the body scent hung clear, pushed slightly to the side by the wind, the ground scent lay in sporadic breaks. He was a man with a big stride.

The trail led down to the lake. Then the man had clambered up the hillside by the public park and walked casually down the tarred main road. At the toll post, with its crowd of holiday-makers, honeymooners, hawkers, vegetable sellers and curio vendors, the trail became disturbed and hazy. I lost it a number of times and found it again. Some people were quite rude. They shouted at Woof to mind his dog and not let it get in the way. Woof and Mohammed, both absorbed in the tracking, answered them as best they could and we continued. Now people began to watch us as though it were some entertainment arranged for them. And indeed it must have seemed like a pantomime or charade for suddenly I stopped and they laughed. I had lost the trail completely. Instead, all I caught was the smell of carbon monoxide.

Woof guessed what had happened. He pointed to the parked taxis and the buses moving past. He shook his head. He patted me. He said to Mohammed, "The man probably took a taxi or boarded a bus."

Mohammed said, "Ya Allah! It is enough. Let us go to my uncle's house and confront him. I shall threaten to kill him, then he will tell the truth."

"Don't be silly," Woof said brusquely, and added, "be patient. The dog hasn't finished his work yet."

Woof took me to the lakeside for a drink of water and I had a short rest while he and Mohammed had a cup of tea in a cafe. Then we hired a boat to the other side of the lake; it saved us walking much of the way back to the scene of the crime.

Woof gave me the scent once more from the stick but this time he asked me to back-track. I was to find out where the man had come from.

I must tell you right away that since working on this case I have checked with others and found that few trained working dogs have been taught this. It entails a far more difficult process, for you have to go back on a trail that is getting colder all the time. It can be most discouraging for a dog who has only been trained to track a smell to its source; back-tracking entails tracing a smell to its origin in time not in space. But again, though the idea is complex and the result sophisticated, the method of learning it is simple. It is based on going back to retrieve dropped objects by smell.

I knew now that Woof was depending on me. I sensed the urgency in his voice. I began going back on the track of the criminal's arrival. It is impossible to tell you how difficult this was for me; I was going, in a manner of speaking, against the grain. All my instincts said, "Forward! Catch the man!" But my mind said, "No, back, back, show the way he came, find anything he dropped along the way; Woof is asking this of you."

The back-trail was so long I might even have given up but then I found something and my heart rejoiced. It was the sole of one of his shoes, his *mojris*! I took it in my mouth and held it up to Woof in triumph. I was bristling all over like a porcupine. It was wonderful to have it confirmed that I was on the right trail by going back; it was wonderful to think that this piece of leather was perhaps what Woof was looking for.

He took it from me and petted me profusely and hugged me.

Then he asked me to continue back-tracking. We moved up, past the entrance to the Mahabaleshwar Club, along the pavement of the road that ran parallel to the bazaar. The man had obviously followed Abdul Rahman quite casually and then struck.

Now we had moved beyond the bazaar and, passing on to the other side, we were entering the jungle again. At this point, Woof stopped me and sent Mohammed off for a pan of water from some shopkeeper in the bazaar. Woof sat on a milestone and smoked. I rested and drank some water. Mohammed went off to return the pan.

Woof had placed the leather sole carefully in a plastic bag which is part of his tracking equipment. Now he renewed my memory of the scent, as Mohammed joined us, and we set off again.

From here it wasn't far to go, but the trail led deep into the woods and we had no light with us. It was getting dark. In a while, we came to a solitary shack in the jungle. Beside it was a covered pen and from this pen came the bleating of sheep. A dog barked by the door of the hut but he was obviously as much of an intruder as we were, for he was relieved to see that we meant him no harm and he quietly slunk away. He was probably one of the jungle-dwelling dogs who had come foraging for scraps. He had barked out of sheer alarm.

We went up to the hut. It was empty. The smell of the criminal was very strong but he was not here. There was no furniture of any kind. The hut was in disuse. Apparently, the criminal was merely camping here. He could be a nomadic shepherd or this might be one of his usual stops when grazing his sheep.

I sniffed about. Suddenly, the old clothes part of the smell was overpowering. I poked about behind some rotten timber and drew out a bundle. Woof opened it. It was an old shirt and a tattered smelly blanket wrapped in a discarded bedcover.

Woof praised me and petted me softly. Then he unclipped the long leash. I searched the room more thoroughly. Woof signalled to me with the closed fist, meaning I should refrain from barking. He said to Mohammed, "We'll wait. He's bound to return soon. The sheep are here."

Outside the sheep went on bleating. Mohammed took out a

knife from his pocket. Woof shook his head.

"None of that," he whispered. "Put it away. If you injure him seriously or kill him, you'll have a hard time proving anything in court. Leave it to Ranjha. He knows what to do."

He signalled me to his side. I lay down beside him. We waited.

An hour or so later I heard some sounds approaching. I nudged Woof and gave a low growl. He patted me on the head. Then he posted Mohammed on the other side of the door.

As I listened, I became aware that I was hearing the footsteps of two people as they came crackling and snapping over the dry leaves and twigs. One of the men seemed to be leading a pony. There are plenty of ponies in Mahabaleshwar but few are ever seen out after dark. The children and holidaymakers are usually snug in their rooms at this time. It must be one of the pony-men.

Woof held up two fingers to Mohammed to indicate that there were two men outside. Mohammed shrugged dolefully in response.

The two men were very slow about coming in. They stood outside for a long time, talking in low whispers. It was getting awfully cold.

We heard a sort of scraping noise as the shepherd undid some kind of barricade on the pen. Then, to our surprise, he sent four sheep scampering into the hut. The sheep were as startled as we were. They bleated and ran about and the most courageous one backed away in front of me and began to stamp her hooves. Woof signalled me to stay still.

This was the shepherd's method of warming his hut for the night. With four sheep sleeping beside him it would be quite cosy. But now the two men hesitated outside, alerted by the stamping hooves.

The shepherd moved carefully to the door. As he stepped on the threshold Woof pulled him in and sent him staggering to the further wall. He was a hefty man in a turban.

Woof shouted, "Ranjha, catch!"

I grabbed the man by his wrist.

Mohammed had run out after the pony-man. Woof dashed out, too. But in all this mêlée the four sheep were causing havoc. It was enough to unnerve me, but I hung on to the hefty man. He cursed and swung and hit out at me but I would not let him go.

Outside there were shouts and the sounds of a scuffle but then I heard the hoofbeats of the pony and I knew the other one had escaped.

Now the shepherd was standing still. He knew he would invite my anger and some danger to himself if he struggled.

"Never mind the other fellow now," Woof said. "We've got the one we want, I think."

Mohammed lit a match and looked at the shepherd's face.

"Ghulam Ahmed!" he exclaimed. "You! Of course, I should have guessed."

"Who is he?" Woof asked.

"Oh, just a good-for-nothing. He pretends he's a shepherd but he'd do anything for a quick rupee, even try to kill my poor old father."

"What are you talking about?" the shepherd asked in a hoarse voice. Then he coughed, spat on the floor and said, "I don't know what you're talking about. I haven't done anything. How dare you come in here and set this dog on me. I'll . . . I'll report you to the police. I'll tell them you're trying to steal my sheep."

Mohammed and the man called Ghulam Ahmed began to curse each other. Woof interrupted. He told Mohammed to stop wasting matches and to return the sheep to the pen. Then they smashed bits of the rotten timber by stamping on it and on the earthen floor of the hut, they lit a fire. All the time I held on to the wrist of the man called Ghulam Ahmed.

"Now," said Woof to the man, "hand over the five hundred rupees you stole and tell us who the pony-man was. Otherwise we'll leave it to the police to find out."

Ghulam Ahmed swore he was innocent. He said, "You can search the hut, you can search me. I haven't got anybody's five hundred rupees."

It was a most convincing performance and if it wasn't for the fact that I had his scent in my nostrils, Woof might have believed him.

Finally, Woof said, "All right, let's take him to the police."

In the shoulder-bag which Ghulam Ahmed was carrying, Woof found a chequered sheet, a torch and some bread. He took the torch and, switching it on, asked me to release Ghulam Ahmed's wrist. Then he commanded me to escort the prisoner. I obeyed, following the man carefully all the way and snarling to dissuade him whenever he seemed like wanting to run. We walked single file, Mohammed in front and Woof bringing up the rear.

The police station is in the centre of the little bazaar but before we could reach it we received a shock for there in the main street was the makings of a riot. Abdul Rahman had been able to hold himself in no longer. He had despaired of our attempts and he had told all to his relatives. The people of the lane in which he lived were infuriated that anyone should have attacked old Abdul Rahman. They agreed that it was more than simple robbery; they were certain, too, that it was all the doing of Suleiman, the strawberry seller and distant cousin of Abdul Rahman. They felt it was dastardly. They had dragged Suleiman before Abdul for a confrontation, and the blood of the younger men on both sides was boiling.

We tried to make our way to the police station but some people shouted, "Here they are! Here they are! They've caught the fellow who was sent to do it."

We were ushered into the centre of the crowd. At the edges of the mob we could see policemen moving into action telling people to break it up. Abdul Rahman rushed towards us; so did Suleiman. We climbed on to the verandah of a shop. The crowd surged forward.

Mohammed held up his hands and shouted over the noise, "We have found the culprit. Here is the robber who tried to kill my father."

The crowd let out a wail of fury.

"Wait!" Mohammed shouted. "As I am the son of my father, I tell you Suleiman sahib had nothing to do with it."

But the crowd now wanted blood. It began to chant, "Kill the robber . . . kill the robber!"

The robber, Ghulam Ahmed, went pale and began to tremble.

The police were trying to reach us but it was difficult with so many people jostling about, smouldering with anger. The crowd was growing. The people nearest us shouted and rushed for the prisoner.

Woof called out, "Ranjha, alert!"

I sprang in front and stood bristling. I had sensed the danger. The front-rankers stopped in dismay. The crowd hesitated. I snarled and showed my fangs. To be frank with you, I was afraid. But it had a sobering effect on the crowd. Three young louts broke towards us but I now turned on them barking and snarling and as each one tried to avoid me the crowd split in panic and spread outwards and back. It began to break up.

The few policemen that Mahabaleshwar normally requires were gaining control of the situation. Two of them reached the prisoner. The crowd murmured and held back. A path was cleared to the police station.

Ghulam Ahmed was deposited there with a quick explanation to the Inspector in charge. Then the Inspector and a constable accompanied us to the stables where all the ponies were kept. Four ponies were still warm. It was impossible to make out which one had been ridden in from the meeting with the shepherd. Enquiries also were of no avail. No one wanted to point a finger at the other; they were, after all, working together in the same stables. The Inspector threatened to jail all four men who had brought in the last ponies.

The men were lined up. They looked at each other and each one denied having anything to do with the robbery.

I was moving about free but close to Woof when suddenly a

combination of powerfully haunting smells struck my nose. I sniffed the air. Woof noticed and encouraged me. He said softly, "Ranjha, pick!"

I knew the command. I moved forward. The four men began to retreat.

"Stand still," Woof said. "He won't harm you—if you're innocent."

The youngest of the men began to tremble. There was a terrible odour of fear. Even in the cool of the night, he was perspiring. And then I knew what the smell was! It was a combination of the scents of Abdul Rahman and the shepherd. It hung in the air. I leaned my nose into it. Yes, there it was, as compelling as the scent of a ripe apple on a tree. I reached out and grabbed the hand that was wearing the ring—the caddie's ring.

The youth broke down and confessed.

"It's uncanny!" said the Inspector and looked at me with amazement. "How did he guess?"

Woof understood, of course. He pointed to the ring on the pony-boy's finger.

"He worked it out from the evidence," Woof said.

The money was recovered from the pony-boy and so were the watch and the hardly-usable pen. The ring was the most important recovery of all, of course, though it was a cheap and worthless thing.

At the police station, the shepherd still denied his part in the robbery. He tried to blame it all on the pony-boy. Woof took out his plastic bag and handed the leather sole to the Inspector.

"That," he said, "came from the *mojri* of the man who tried to kill the caddie."

The shepherd frowned and looked down and curiosity overcame him. He lifted one foot, then the other. One of the soles was missing. He shook his head in bewilderment and then he asked, "How did you know?"

Woof merely pointed at me and smiled.

The shepherd sighed, sat down on the bench, nodded and

said, "I did it. We planned it together—the pony-boy and I. We followed old Abdul to the golf-course, then I tied my turban round my face and did it."

Later, at the wedding of Abdul Rahman's daughter I was garlanded like a guest of honour. Both Suleiman and Abdul Rahman made little speeches and then, for the first time in public, I was called Dog Detective Ranjha.

7

The Case of the Washerman's Sheets

Many cases now followed. People heard of us. They would come to us for help. We always went. And it never mattered to me whether it was a big case or a small one. I looked as eagerly for the lost toy of a child as for an absconding murderer.

The most delicate and tricky of the minor cases was the one which people thought I had not been able to solve. We called it the Case of the Washerman's Sheets.

Someone had stolen a pair of sheets which the *dhobi*, or washerman, had put out to dry on some rocks by the river. The poor old man was most upset. The sheets were expensive. They belonged to one of his clients. He couldn't afford to replace them. What was he to do?

It was too small a matter to bring to the notice of the police. So he came to us.

We went to the riverbank. It was a popular place with washermen; there were hundreds of them there, each with his own reserved section of the riverbank. The rocks were blanketed with a colourful patchwork of many clothes.

Woof was aghast to see so many people. It seemed a very difficult task to track a thief from among all the washermen there. Woof was certain that one of them had casually included the missing sheets in his own bundle. But he was wrong. The thief was not another washerman.

But there's no denying that finding the culprit put me to great effort. To begin with, there was no way of my taking the scent except off the ground. Then, Woof made the mistake of making me smell the spot where the sheets had been spread. Now the smell on the sheets naturally belonged to the old fellow who had washed the sheets, so I raced off and grabbed hold of the poor old washerman!

He screamed and tried to run for he was sorely frightened. But I held him fast, tearing his coat in the process. Woof understood what had happened and came running up and asked me to release him. By now the washerman was wailing, "O God, what have I done to deserve this? I am robbed and then the animal who is to catch the thief accuses me! Woe is me, I'm shamed before everyone!"

Woof couldn't help laughing nor could the other washermen who had gathered round.

Anyway, back we went to the rocks where the sheets had been dried and this time Woof put me to sniffing about the little grassy path that led into the jungle. I caught a scent, of course, and it was just a chance that it belonged to the thief. Mingled with the scent of the man was the faint whiff of the washed sheets, but Woof had no way of knowing this, so when I started to circle round and head towards the bazaar, he tried to pull me off the scent. But now I was not inclined to give up. Fortunately, Woof let me continue when he realised I was keen to go on. What was troubling Woof most was that as we moved nearer to the area of the bazaar a crowd of curious urchins and others tagged on behind us. And the crowd kept growing like a rolling snowball.

Soon we were in a little shantytown. This being a hilly place, the houses were constructed on different levels. At the very top, above this maze of narrow lanes and streets, was the bazaar. All kinds of inquisitive questions were being asked behind us. Were we the police? Or were we acting a scene for a film and if so who were the leading stars and where were they? We felt a bit like a travelling entertainment for the idle. And I could sense that Woof was becoming tense and irritable.

Just then I turned into a house where the scent of the man was strong but stronger still was the smell of the sheets. Going in, I found no one. Everyone in the area seemed to be out, behind me! But the scent was more than strong, it was fierce and powerful. I went to some sacks, trying to locate the origin of the smell of the sheets, but the sacks only contained coal. Then I went to a trunk under the bed but it only had other clothes. As I moved along one of the walls, the smell hung above me. I looked up. A bag was hanging on a peg. I leaped up. Yes, the smell was quite concentrated here but like a recurring memory. I took the bag between my teeth. Woof slipped it off the peg. I knew he was feeling diffident, intruding like this into someone's house in the middle of a populous area. I hoped the evidence I was giving him would reassure him but it didn't. He had no way of knowing the smell that emanated from the bag. I watched him examine it. It was a postman's satchel and it was empty.

But just as he was about to turn away in disillusionment, I began to scratch at the doors of a cupboard. With a sigh and a shrug, Woof pulled open the door. It contained clothes but now the smell of the sheets was hitting me like a charge of dynamite up my nostrils. One side of the cupboard had some shirts on hangers but the scent was exploding at me from floor-level. I pushed my snout into a bundle and nosed and came out holding a corner of one of the sheets. The washerman who had stayed close to Woof all this time shouted, "That's it!"

Woof said nothing till we were outside, then he casually asked the people who were gathered there, "Whose house is this?"

A number of them answered, "Z.A. Farooqi, the postman."

Woof frowned, nodded and came back indoors. He seemed worried. Once, when the washerman tried to go out, he restrained him with a grip on his arm. Finally, he said to the washerman, "Look, we've tried to help you—"

"You have!" the man exclaimed. "You've found my sheets. Now we just have to go on and catch the thief. He must have seen us coming and run away. But you'll catch him, I know you will."

"We'll catch him, yes. But I don't think it will help matters."

"What do you mean?"

" I mean that it's a dangerous situation. We know he's guilty. But there's a large crowd outside."

"So what? They're all good people. They would be happy if we caught a thief."

"No doubt. But there are always some nasty persons in such a crowd. You're a Hindu and he's a Muslim."

"How does that matter?"

"Unfortunately, it does to some people and I think, in the interest of the good of the people, we must not give the rotten element in both communities such a chance."

Woof was right. It was better not to cause a commotion that might involve crowds of people. A Hindu-Muslim episode can develop into an incident like a Protestant-Catholic episode in Ireland. So Woof swore the washerman to secrecy but promised him that he would get his sheets back. The washerman was pleased enough at the outcome—after all, he only wanted his sheets back.

We left the house pretending that we had been mistaken, and we walked the length of the bazaar as though we were still tracking, in order to throw the crowd off the scent! Then we trailed off to a lame end at the point where we had begun—the riverbank! By then it was nearing ten o'clock and most of the crowd had wearied and dispersed.

The next day Woof located Farooqi, the postman. Farooqi, of course, realised that he had been found out and was thankful he wasn't being handed over to the police. He was really quite a good person. He was man enough to confess that he had picked up the sheets when passing by the riverbank. He had stuffed them into his satchel and walked on home. It was the first and only temptation of this kind which he had ever given in to all his life. He asked to be forgiven.

Woof was touched by his ability to make a clean breast of the matter. Within the hour, Farooqi brought the sheets to Woof and Woof returned them to the washerman.

It made me realise that sometimes the obvious solution is not always the correct answer to the situation.

In a quite different way, the obvious solution was not the correct answer in the case that began when I found a hidden earring. It lay in the shallow knot-hole of a tree. I don't remember now whether I drew Woof's attention to it with a bark or whether he saw me raise my tail a few degrees in excitement and came to my side to see. Anyway, there it was, a gold earring with three emeralds glinting like the eyes of some weird insect. Naturally, we set off to return it to the person who had left it there. It seemed the obvious thing to do and we hardly realised then that this was not the correct answer to the situation. For, you see, we were taking it back not to the owner but to the thief who had hidden it.

That was the beginning of the Case of the Hidden Earring.

8

The Case of the Hidden Earring

*T*he tree in which I found the hidden earring grew in the grounds of the Missionary's bungalow. I was merely poking about as any tracker dog might when I was struck by the strong smell of soap coming from the knot-hole of a tree. It was quite an ordinary tree but the soapy smell was extraordinary. And it was not the smell of toilet soap either; it was the smell of a washing powder used for cleaning clothes. As I caught the unexpected odour I could almost see the flakes dissolving and foaming in a bucket of water.

I put my nose into the knot-hole and took out the earring. Woof gasped. The three large emeralds glittered on their background of gold.

Woof took the earring from me and said, "Let's return it."

As I set off, tracking free, with my nose to the ground, I knew Woof was thinking, as I was, that it was a funny place in which to find an earring. What was perhaps even funnier was that it wasn't a pair of earrings but just one. How had it come to be there?

The Missionary's bungalow was a gaunt, deserted house. We

had never seen a missionary there yet but then perhaps that was just an old name for the crumbling ruin. Mahabaleshwar is full of such places—solitary, uncared for, almost forgotten. I often heard Woof asking passing villagers about these neglected bungalows scattered like milestones of history amid the jungle. But no one could tell us more than that sometimes their owners would come from the cities on a short holiday and camp in those cold, unfurnished rooms only to return to the city in disgust and there sell the structure to some to other person who would rarely come.

For a moment I wondered what we would do if the scent led up to the Missionary's bungalow for I knew there was no one there now. The trail was two days old.

But we went on past the bungalow and down a path leading to some huts. Had we been moving merely instinctively, we might have rushed straight into that cluster of huts and asked about for the owner of the earring. We were, however, following a definite trail and the scent led off to the right. Behind me Woof stopped in puzzlement. I had sniffed my way off the path now and was inching up the hill into the woods.

I could understand Woof's puzzlement. After all, there was a road going round the woods. Why hadn't the person we were following taken the open road? Even the little paths that crisscrossed the jungle had been avoided. It was almost as if the earring had been deposited there in stealth; the person had been to the tree and then slipped away through the jungle like a thief.

It is difficult for me to stop and think once I am set on the trail of something or someone. I gave my short, impatient call which is half howl, half moan. Woof saw that my tail was curving up and my hair bristling in excitement; he understood that I was on the track. Human beings sometimes need to be reassured that you are not misleading them. With a shrug and a shake of his head, Woof followed.

We made our way through bramble and fern and past bushes of the yellow wildflower known in these parts as *dingler*. Every now and again, Woof called out to me to wait for him. Tracking free, without the restraint of a harness, I was moving fast and well ahead. The scent was strong and getting stronger for here, in the woods, the wind had not blown it away and the sun had not been able to reach in and destroy it. There was a stale, rotting touch to it, of course; to me it was as clear as the odour of a bad egg in a windless room.

Then we were out in a clearing and going down a slight incline and crossing a road. The road, the incline, the clearing—all seemed familiar to me and yet, for the moment, I couldn't place them. I tried not to think of where we were, my job was to concentrate on the tracking. Now the smell had developed a fresher, sweet overtone. I recognized it as an attar, a kind of cloying perfume. This particular attar was obviously an extract of roses. It was heady and overpowering. It flowed up my nose and blossomed like roses in my nostrils. I sneezed, shook my head clear and rubbed at my muzzle with a paw. Woof began to wonder if I was getting a cold!

Under the smell of roses lay the smell of soap and body odour. And covering it all like a wrapper over a toffee was the smell of wood-smoke. So it was clear that the person I was tracking used perfume, washed clothes and cooked over a wood-fire. And considering that I had taken the scent from an earring, it was fairly obvious that I was trailing a woman. The body odour, too, confirmed this, for men and women smell different from each other. But, of course, Woof had no way yet of knowing all this.

We were now crossing an unkempt, untidy grass verge and heading towards a hut. I looked up now and saw that we were in the large compound of a bungalow. The hut stood at the end of the compound.

It was unnecessary now to keep my nose to the ground-scent, for the body-scent was like a canal of honey in the air. I kept my head up and into it, pulled along like a paper boat by a current.

Tracking can be so enjoyable that a dog loses himself in the delicious symphony of smells as they grow clearer and engulf him in a cloud of ecstasy. That is what happened to me. Foolish as it may seem, I rushed on in my enthusiasm past the woman who had stepped out of the hut and was now hanging clothes out to dry on a line.

Suddenly I realised I had overshot the source of the scent. I turned round, feeling quite silly. I went up to the thin, tired-looking, sari-clad woman and gently held her wrist in my mouth. Then I stepped back a pace and barked. Woof came up to the woman and held out the earring to her.

Instead of being delighted and thankful, she gasped and went white as a sheet.

Woof smiled and took another step forward but she withdrew, trembling, and dropped the clothes she was holding. One of her hands went to her mouth and it seemed as though she was trying to stop herself from screaming. In a second she was perspiring and there was a terrible smell of fear in the air.

Woof mistook her reaction for surprise. He said kindly, "We found it in a tree by the Missionary's Bungalow."

"No, no, no!" she cried. "I didn't put it there. I don't know anything about it!"

Woof was taken aback. He looked at me. I barked at the woman. I knew for certain that it was she who had hidden the earring there. But I could see that Woof was more inclined to believe a human being than a dog. He seemed disappointed in me as if I had made some mistake!

At this point a tall villager dressed in a Gandhi cap and clean white clothes appeared at the door of the hut. The woman ran to him breathlessly and said, pointing at Woof, "Look! He's got that lady's earring. He says I hid it in some tree. He's accusing me!"

The man took a couple of steps towards Woof and looked down at him with his head cocked slightly to one side. He spoke in a nasty tone.

"Who're you?" he asked.

Woof had by now sensed that something was wrong. He

realised that the earring in his hand was a stolen one. The woman recognized it but wished to deny all knowledge of how it came to be in the knot-hole of a tree.

Woof said, "Never mind who I am. Take me to the owner of this earring."

The tall man looked at the woman. Then he looked at me. Turning to Woof, he asked, "Is that a police dog?"

"No," Woof said, "but he's trained like one. He tracked this woman here. She stole the earring, I think, and hid it in the tree."

"Look, mister," the man said, "you are not a policeman to be going around accusing people. I happen to be the *patil*, the head-man of Mangli village down in the valley. I am appointed by the police. I know the law and I know who is a thief and who is not. This woman is my wife. Your dog has no business to go about chasing innocent people. Such a dog is a danger and a nuisance. He should be shot. Now give me the earring and I shall return it to its owner."

"No," said Woof, "I'll take it back to the owner myself."

"I am not a man to be trifled with," the tall fellow said, removing his cap and dusting it forcefully against one hand.

The slapping sound irritated me. It was a threat of violence. He was that kind of a man. I growled.

The *patil* put the cap back on his head, turned on his heel and went into the hut.

Woof sighed and motioning me to his side began to walk away.

The woman called something to the man and now he came back to the door of his hut. In his hand was a double-barrel gun.

"Hey you!" the man shouted. "Where're you going?"

Woof turned round.

"To the police," he said.

"No," said the man, "you are not. I say you are not."

I could see that the sight of the gun had not only shocked and frightened Woof, it had also made him angry.

"Surely," Woof said in an incredulous voice, "you don't intend to use that silly thing simply because I am going to the police with a stolen earring!"

"This silly thing," the *patil* said sarcastically, "is a loaded twelve-bore. It helps me keep peace in the village. It also enables me to hunt rabbits. But today I could use it to destroy a dangerous dog and recover a stolen earring from his master."

Woof gave a little laugh.

"No one will believe you," he said.

"You won't be around to worry about that," the man replied, "and I have ways of making people believe me. You know what I think? I think you are trying to frame my wife. I think you are accusing her falsely in order to ruin my family name. This is a trick of my enemies. They have got you to do this for them. Perhaps you are innocent of mischief, I grant that. Perhaps you have been misled. You don't look the kind of a person to get involved in the politics of a little local village. But who knows? The world is full of strange people. You may be a member of some political party that's trying to gain control of the area. You may be helping some people to dislodge me from my position as *patil* of the village."

Woof was aghast. "You must be crazy!" he said.

The man nodded. "Maybe I am. Maybe I'm clever. Maybe I'm anything. Just give me the earring and get out of here. You're a young man. Don't mess up your life by poking your nose into other people's business."

"Be reasonable," Woof said with an attempt at a smile. "The dog and I happened to find a piece of jewellery and we want only to do the right thing by returning it to the owner."

The man cocked both barrels of his gun and muttered, "I've told you—just give it to me and get out."

His eyes had gone red and he was again looking at us sideways across his hawk-like nose. The woman clung to one of his arms but he now shrugged her aside and raised the gun. It pointed at me.

"All right," Woof said. "Here you are, take the earring."

But the man was no fool. He jerked his head and said, "Throw it at my feet."

Woof hesitated. Then he said, "No, one of the emeralds is loose. It'll fall out."

"Never mind," said the man. "If the stone falls out, we'll find it."

"As you wish," Woof said and threw the earring at his feet. The man did not even look down.

"Now, I want you to—" he began but before he could say more Woof pointed to a spot near his feet.

"By the way," Woof said, "is that a snake crawling into your hut?"

There *are* snakes in Mahabaleshwar but the poisonous kinds are rare. Nevertheless, people have to be careful, especially in the rainy season and soon after. And snakes sometimes do crawl into huts.

The man shifted on his feet and quickly looked down.

"Ranjha, disarm!" Woof shouted and rushed forward.

A dog is always faster than a man. I had leapt past Woof and straight at the *patil* before he could look up. As I threw him to the ground and took the cold steel of the gun in my jaws, a thunderous explosion shook the barrel. I had half wrenched the gun out of the man's hand but now it went flying with the force of the bang. I was also flung aside. I had been trained not to be afraid of gunfire or crackers but I had never known the roar and power of a gun going off while I was holding it. The terrible noise and the effect of it was so awesome that for a moment I thought I was dying. As I got up, dazed and deafened, I saw that the man was getting up too. The woman was screaming. Woof was moaning on the ground.

I went straight to Woof and sniffed at him and licked his face. I forgot everything else. I was terrified that Woof was hurt. Perhaps it was a mistake to worry just then about Woof but I couldn't help it. I didn't mind being shot and killed but I had to

see to Woof. The gun was lying by Woof's head. It looked as if he had been struck by the wooden butt.

The woman was shouting and screaming. She had picked up a thick chunk of firewood and was coming towards me. Her husband was now picking up the gun.

Woof said weakly, "Attack." And then he closed his eyes and slumped. I sniffed at him. He was breathing all right. He was just unconscious. He had asked me to attack. That was the ultimate command I could be given. That meant Woof was in grave danger. I had to do everything I could to save him. I had to prevent them from injuring Woof. It took me less than a second to act on Woof's command.

But worried as I was, I was too late.

The woman hit me with the chunk of wood. She must have been quite unnerved by events or perhaps she was frightened of me. She missed my head and the blow caught me on the back. I snarled and jumped. I had her by the arm and hung on. She shrieked and tried to pry me loose but I had been trained to hang on even if I was lifted off the ground and whirled in a circle. The man had the gun now and was shouting to her but he couldn't fire because he was afraid of hitting her. Then I became aware of people running towards us from the big house and some were running along the road.

The woman fainted and fell down. I released her. As I turned, I saw that Woof was trying to sit up and the man was about to shoot at me.

Woof gasped, "Ranjha, down!"

There was such urgency in his voice though it was low that I immediately flopped down. Just then there was another deafening explosion and something whistled over my head.

The man clicked open the barrel and threw down two smoking cartridge cases, then he ran towards the hut. He was going for more ammunition but by now four or five people had arrived on the scene. He seemed undecided whether to stay or run. Then, amazingly, he sat down on a step and putting the gun aside took his head in his hands. People were gathering round now and asking what was happening. He said nothing.

They helped Woof to get up and they threw cold water on the woman's face and revived her.

They looked at me, still in the 'down' position, and wondered whether I was to blame for the trouble. Some said aloud that I had probably been raiding the man's chickens, others said that I had most likely attacked the woman for no reason.

"What a lovely dog!" a child's voice said quite inappropriately at that moment. I looked and saw that three well-dressed children had come along with their parents from the house at the farther end of the compound.

While the father of the children stepped into the centre of the growing circle and asked, "What's going on here?" one of the children made friendly noises in my direction. Even in the 'down' position, I couldn't help wagging my tail. It thumped the ground. That made the children laugh. I began to feel more relaxed. They came up and began to pet me. I felt better. At least someone in the crowd seemed to be on my side.

Woof was explaining what had happened. The father of the children listened and then said, "I must thank you for what you've done. I've never really trusted this fellow or his wife. He's supposed to be the gardener of this bungalow but he spends all his time being the terror of his village in the valley. His wife does the washing for the house. We've been losing odd bits of jewellery ever since we bought this place and started coming up for the school holidays. Somehow we could never work up the courage to sack this couple. This fellow is such a bully around here that I was . . . well, in a way, frightened of accusing them on mere suspicion. By the way, allow me to introduce myself. My name is Desai. My wife. My children."

Mrs Desai joined her palms and greeted Woof and thanked him.

Mr Desai said that on hearing the first gunshot he had phoned the police. He said he was going to hand the gardener and his wife over to the police.

Now the gardener stood up and looked down at everyone across the bridge of his nose.

"What a lot of rubbish is being talked!" he said. "What accusations are being flung! What threats of action against a poor, innocent man and his wife! If Mr Desai wants me to leave his employ, I will. My wife and I will go away this very minute. But I will not have my good name tarnished. The police know me to be an honest man. The name of my family is being threatened for other reasons. This is a frame-up. Mr Desai is against me for certain deep reasons which I shall explain later. I know things about him. That is why he wants to ruin my good name. No jewellery was ever lost as far as I know. This is the first time I'm hearing of it. For that matter, where *is* this precious earring that is supposed to have been brought back by this young man?"

The police had arrived in the middle of this speech and now an Inspector came forward and took charge of the situation.

The crowd had grown and was murmuring.

Mrs Desai was exclaiming at the amazing audacity of the gardener in trying to lie his way out of the whole thing. Mr Desai was spluttering and fuming.

Woof made a full statement of what had happened. The Inspector listened to all that was being said. When Woof gave his name, the Inspector said, "Ah yes, I've heard of you and your dog. I wasn't on duty the night of the riot in the bazaar but my colleagues have told me how you helped. Now, the first thing, of course, is—where is the earring which you say you found?"

Everyone began to scan the ground for the earring.

The gardener said, "There's no point looking for the ornament. It doesn't exist. It's all a lot of lies to put me in a bad light with my people."

The Inspector called out to everybody to stay where they were. Then he began to look around by the hut for the earring. The gardener laughed sarcastically.

After a couple of minutes he said, "I know you would like to believe this young man but it's just not true. He never threw any earring or whatever on the ground."

Now one of the children said, "He's a liar. We know that Mummy's lost a lot of things. She lost an earring two days ago."

"Ah ha," said the gardener, "she may have lost these things. I'm not denying that. She may have lost them through carelessness while walking in the bazaar or during a walk. I have never seen this famous earring nor has my wife."

The children too began to cast their eyes over the ground. In the grass and the soft earth, it was difficult to see any trace of an earring.

"Excuse me, Inspector," Woof said. "May I suggest that we ask the dog to search for it?"

"The dog!" the Inspector exclaimed. "How would he find it?"

"There is a way," said Woof.

"Don't tell me he knows the meaning of the word *earring*!"

"No, Inspector, he doesn't. He places as much value on an earring as on a piece of wood or a bit of stone. But I've just thought of a way by which he can find it."

"Hm. All right. No harm in trying. And if there is such an earring about, at least he won't be tempted to pocket it!"

"Ranjha, come," Woof called.

I went to him. He cupped his hands over my nose, giving me his own scent; then he asked me to seek and fetch. I began to sniff the ground in the direction in which he pointed.

"I see," said the Inspector. "Very clever. Quite sensible. Since you threw the earring and since you carried it all the way here, it'll still have your scent on it."

"Right," said Woof and I imagine he must have smiled but I didn't look at him to find out; I was busy with the task I had been set.

I sniffed over the patch of ground and in a few seconds I located the spot where the object had lain. But it had been moved—perhaps by the scrambling about during the struggle, or perhaps because someone had picked it up. Close by was the step on which the gardener had sat with his head in his hands. The smell of the gardener's footwear was mingled with Woof's scent on the spot where the earring had been. That meant the gardener had placed his feet close to or over the earring. However, my job was just to sniff; the conclusions were to be left to Woof. So I continued to sniff about in widening circles. I was sniffing various shoes and sandals and feet now. Woof assured people that there was no risk to them. They stood still. But as I approached the shoes of the gardener, he began to move and complain against me.

"This dog is dangerous, I tell you. He attacked me and then he attacked my wife. He . . . he . . . he . . . don't let him come near me!"

He was moving about, taking short steps. It annoyed me. I knew now that the earring was tucked between his left foot and the *mojri* he was wearing. It must have hurt the sole of his foot. I suppose he'd picked up the earring with his bare foot, taking it up between his toes, while he sat there on the step. Now I made a determined grab for his *mojri*. It came off and out tumbled the earring. I carried it to Woof.

The children burst into spontaneous applause. My tail couldn't help wagging. Everyone else joined in with the children and clapped. It was like being at some kind of public demonstration.

"I hope the applause doesn't go to his head!" Woof said, laughing.

People were chuckling and murmuring, but all this while, the gardener had been sidling away. No one expected him to make a run for it. After all, his wife was still there standing in the verandah of their quarters. But perhaps some kind of panic seized him; perhaps he had decided to abandon his wife to her fate. If they had stolen many things over the years, they must have a tidy sum hidden away somewhere. Perhaps his intention was to escape out of the district entirely.

Anyway, he didn't get far, not even as far as the clearing

beyond the road. Everyone took off after him but being a tall man with a big stride he easily outpaced them. Then Woof said, quite casually now, "Ranjha, arrest!" and waved me in the fleeing gardener's direction.

As I said before, a dog is much faster than human beings.

I must admit that the applause this time did go a little to my head. I leapt all over the children and adults as they petted me and I kissed them.

Later, when Wuff heard about it all she gave me a special reward for having stood by Woof. The snack she served me in my bowl is the one I consider the most delicious treat—chicken livers on toast. That's my very favourite.

9

The Case of the Dancing Ghost

*T*here were days when Wuff worried terribly about Woof's safety and mine. There were nights she spent sleepless, wondering what dangers we were facing. There were occasions when she was inclined to put her foot down and make us refuse a case. But she never did. Somehow adventure seemed to have become a part of family life.

Over the months, Wuff had become accustomed to our going off on a track with just a word to her. Much of the time, of course, she was busy with the baby and the housework but she had nevertheless begun to take a bemused interest in my progress. In the beginning, I think, she had taken it for granted that Woof's training of me was a kind of idiosyncrasy, a sort of quirk—writers are especially known to be full of them, and Woof had his full share, I can assure you!

Gradually, however, Wuff had come to see that I was indeed becoming a highly-trained and capable working dog. But while she was there at the beginning and end of each case, she never had to actually accompany us on one. So, like the clear-headed person she is, she took my growing renown without too much fuss. To her, I remained really just the family dog. What pleased her most was that I could carry some of the shopping in a basket or amuse the baby, who was now toddling about, by retrieving sticks thrown in a lake.

During our family walks, the baby was often carried in a back-pack like an open haversack and the child would accidentally drop things such as a bonnet or a sweater; it was I who always went back for them, locating the objects by scent, and when I returned them to Wuff, she would pet me and that was like a ton of praise to me.

In particular, Wuff liked it that if the baby sat astride me while I was lying down, and bounced about on my back as though I were a rocking-horse, I never got up or threw her off. But perhaps what amused Wuff most of all was that when Woof was busy at his writing, he would often send her a note, carried by me in my mouth, asking for the umpteenth cup of tea. In short, let me put it this way—I had a happy, contented home life and tried to be a useful member of the household.

It was on one such carefree day at home, while Wuff was involved in bathing the baby, that we were invited to solve a rather weird kind of mystery—the Case of the Dancing Ghost.

It all began with a visit to us of a fat, round man in a suit smelling of petrol. Obviously, his suit had just been drycleaned. As he sat in a cane chair in the garden talking to Woof, I sniffed him and he eyed me with a kind of wary interest.

"Don't worry," Woof said, "that's just his way of getting ac-quainted. He sniffs everyone he meets."

The fair-complexioned fat man quivered like   jelly and gave a blubbery sort of laugh.

"Oh I'm not worried," he said. "I love dogs. In fact, it's be-cause of him that I've come to see you."

"Oh?"

"My name is Dr Modi," said the man, handing Woof his card. "I'm hoping to set up a sanatorium for convalescing patients on a large property between Panchgani and Mahabaleshwar. I'm being offered the place quite cheap. It has a beautiful old rambling house on it and a magnificent view. Thirty-seven acres altogether."

"It sounds good," said Woof.

"Yes, just what I need. My patients will be delighted with it. Many of them are suffering from nervous complaints brought on by the pressures of city life. They'll find it most restful. But there is a problem."

"Ah."

"The place is said to be haunted. With a . . . er . . . ghost prancing about, my patients would be reduced to nervous wrecks."

"No doubt," Woof said. "But what sort of a ghost is this supposed to be?"

"Rather an attractive one. A female ghost of great beauty." Dr Modi indulged in another blubbery laugh and gave me a friendly pat. His hand smelt of carbolic soap and Old Spice aftershave lotion.

"Has anyone ever seen this ghost?"

"Oh yes," said Dr Modi and now he took out a cologned handkerchief and dabbed at his brow. "The fact is, I've seen her myself."

"What!"

Dr Modi nodded. "A pale sinuous figure dancing naked in the moonlight, holding a severed head in her hand."

Woof looked carefully at Dr Modi for some time. Then he asked, "And is there some weird story behind this occurrence?"

"Of course. There always is, isn't there? People in the village of Gohad, which is about two miles away, say that it's the ghost of a young English lady who discovered one night that her brother had been murdered and beheaded. They say that she became hysterical and ran about in a state of undress, holding aloft the head of her brother. Poor woman!"

"Surely you don't think the story is true?"

"Well," Dr Modi laughed uncomfortably now, "I've seen the ghost so I suppose I must believe the story. The house is pretty old. Its style and architecture are British. Various British families lived there during the course of the last century and a half. Who can tell what took place in all that time or what didn't? Legends are sometimes the residue of history."

A servant carried out a tray of tea and set it down on the cane table. Dr Modi sipped at his cup thoughtfully. Woof pursed his lips and continued to stir his tea.

After a while, Dr Modi said, "The sanatorium will need to employ people locally. We'll need sweepers, gardeners, maidservants. But no one from the village of Gohad is prepared to come and work there."

"Perhaps they prefer to do their own farming or whatever."

"Oh no, that's not it. They need jobs. They're only too happy to work in an American establishment half a mile away. And they work for some of the bigger strawberry farms in the neighbourhood."

"Hm. You said you had come to see us because of Ranjha. May I ask what you had in mind?"

"I'd like you to investigate this ghost. I thought of going to the police, but I'd look very silly, wouldn't I? I mean, they'd think me mad to be complaining about a ghost!"

"When does this thing appear? Does it have a preference for certain timings and certain nights?"

"I'm afraid not. It could appear any night, any time." Dr Modi put down his cup of tea and laughed again. He added, "It would be easier if it was like other ghosts and came on the stroke of midnight or only on full moon nights."

Woof didn't seem too keen on spending his nights in some lonely spot waiting for a creature that might not appear. Sensing this, Dr Modi took out a cheque book and wrote out a cheque. He handed it to Woof who looked at it in some surprise.

"Please," said Dr Modi, "accept this as half the fee. I'm giving this to you in advance so that you realise that I'm prepared to pay even if it turns out to be a waste of your time. But I assure you, this is not a wild goose chase. The ghost exists and it must be laid to rest once and for all or I shall never be able to open my sanatorium there."

Woof said, "Dr Modi, this is a large amount. Ranjha and I are not really professionals. We just enjoy solving mysteries."

"As far as I'm concerned you are professionals from now on. Frankly, if you also saw the ghost, it would reassure me. You see, I'm beginning to doubt my own sanity. If that sight could so frighten me, imagine what it would do to my patients!"

"And if I do see the ghost, then?"

"You must track it down."

"Track a ghost!"

"You can try."

- "Yes, we can try. Sounds interesting. We've never tracked a ghost before."

All that sounded wonderful on a warm afternoon. But it was a different story waiting out in the cold, night after night, with the wind whistling eerily through the tall dry grass on thirty seven acres of terraced, deserted land. In the moonlight everything looked strange. In the distance, on the top of the hill, the rambling house sprawled like a monster asleep. The branches of a tree waving seemed like a panther about the leap; the surface of the cement tennis court near the house looked like a shimmering pool of water. Something of Woof's nervousness also communicated itself to me. I often swivelled round fiercely, only to find that the sound had been made by falling leaves. Sometimes I was ready to attack and sometimes to run. I could feel my legs trembling under me. I felt sleeping a few times like but the chill wintry air pinched at my nose and limbs. Woof and I snuggled together for warmth. But out there in the open, sheltered only by the soughing grass, there was no question of relaxing. I hated those nights. They made me far too tense. Once Woof accidentally touched my tail and I spun round and had his hand in my mouth before I realised it was his. We heard the jackals and the hyenas, but they must have smelt my presence for they didn't

dare approach. On the third night, there was a coughing sound like that of a panther. Woof heard it too. We moved quietly towards our car which was parked in a thicket. From then on we sat in the car and waited. Woof had brought along biscuits for me and a flask of coffee for himself and the waiting became more bearable.

On the fifth night, we saw her. She was dancing on the hard surface of the tennis court and she had in her hands, as Dr Modi had said, a severed head.

Woof gave a little gasp and froze. He couldn't take his eyes off the swirling figure. It was a maniacal kind of dance. Sometimes she set the head down and swayed and leaped about over it; sometimes she held it up and turned like a top. Her hair swam in the air, floating behind her like weeds in a river. It was graceful and terrible at the same time.

I nudged Woof with my nose. He seemed to have forgotten why we were there. He gave a little jump in his seat. Then, recovering, he sighed with relief, petted me once and quietly opened the door for me. He whispered, "Arrest!"

I slipped out and raced through the high, swishing grass. I was moving by instinct rather than sight. I jumped from terrace to terrace, making as directly as I could for the tennis court.

She must have seen the movement in the grass for when I got there she had vanished.

I charged over the cement surface, criss-crossing it a number of times in a panic of eagerness. In my haste, I forgot for a moment the most elementary part of my training. I should have stayed calm and immediately used my nose.

Now I heard the car door open in the distance and Woof shouting as loudly as he could, "Ranjha, scent! Track! Arrest!"

I heard him and stopped. And put my nose to the ground and started meandering in search of a scent. Yes, there it was. Very strong. A human scent. A female scent, mixed with a smell of paint and paper. Suddenly, wham! I was up against a football-sized object on the ground. It was the severed head.

I touched it with a paw. It rolled over, hollow. It was made of papier-mache, and of course it carried the scent of the woman who had been dancing with it in her hands.

The woman must be hiding somewhere in the darkness, watching me. From the shadows of the house, I heard a gasp and then a scream. I must have seemed pretty frightening myself—a big black-and-tan shape bounding about and then snuffling towards her in the blindness of the night. I could hear her scrambling about now, and then there was the sound of breaking glass and a window being opened and someone wriggling in.

Like a fish being reeled in on a line, I was drawn straight to the window.

She began to scream now, in English, "Help! Help!"

I started to clamber in but she shut the window in my face. I fell back. The next time I sprang straight at the window. The flimsy wooden network broke and more glass shattered. But now she had the back of a chair against the window.

Woof drove up in the car and got out. I barked to let him know that she was inside. He kept the headlights on full beam. A pale, trembling face appeared at the window.

"Thank God," she said. "It's only a dog. I thought it was a panther!"

Woof patted me and asked me to relax. Then he helped her out. She was no ghost. She was very much flesh and blood. She was bleeding on her arm and had two splinters of glass in it. Woof removed the splinters and gave her medicine from the first-aid kit in the car.

She was a middle-aged American lady dressed in skin-coloured ballet tights.

"What on earth were you doing?" Woof asked.

She seemed a little embarrassed but she explained that she lived in the American establishment run by a semi-religious order, a short distance from there. She had been in India three years now and had come "to get away from it all" after a car accident had damaged one of her legs. She had been a ballet dancer and the accident had deprived her of the chance of opening on Broadway in a show called *Herod*. She was to have played the female lead, Salome. The show never opened because the backers pulled out after her accident.

"No wonder you looked so familiar just now," Woof said. "I read about your accident. The papers were full of your photographs and comments about how a great career had been ruined."

"Well—" she grinned a little sadly—"I guess I haven't quite given up hope. I had to get away from all that crippling publicity. And here, where no one could see me, I thought I'd practice the part of Salome. Maybe I could still surprise them one day."

"Why not? You still might," said Woof sympathetically. "But why choose such a deserted place as this? And why rehearse at night? I understand that it's difficult for you to perform the dance of the seven veils in the midst of a semi-religious order but—"

"It's not that," she protested. "They're quite sweet really. It's just that they'd think me crazy. I mean, I should give up, shouldn't I? After all, I've a permanently injured leg! But I'm going on."

"Right," Woof said. "Right. But, if you don't mind my saying so, this is not New York. You can't traipse about here at night. They really might be a panther or two around."

She nodded and said, "Your dog reminded me of that." She ruffled my hair and tugged at my neck affectionately then she sighed and added, "But, you know, New York is far less safe than this place. You couldn't go about alone at night there because of the human beings. There are muggings and crimes and—"

Woof interrupted her with a laugh. He said, "I think I have an ideal solution to your problem. You'll be able to patch up your nerves and rehearse at the same time. You'll be able, if you like, to rehearse right here."

"Say on," she said.

"The well-known specialist, Dr Modi, is turning this place into a sanatorium for convalescents. It could open within a week."

"Gee, that's a great idea! How do I meet this Dr Modi?"

"Leave that to me. He'll be delighted to meet the ghost."

"The ghost? What ghost?"

Woof explained.

She couldn't stop laughing. Eventually she said, "And I thought no one could see me here! I had no idea I was striking terror into the district."

"There is one thing I'd still like to ask you," said Woof. "How did you seem to appear and disappear?"

"Did I? I've no idea."

"From a distance that's how it seemed. One second you were there, another you were not."

"Hold it!" she exclaimed. "I've got it! It must've been my black cape and hood."

She reached in through the window and pulled out her cape. It was a dark woollen one. As she wrapped it round herself and donned the hood, she seemed to merge with the night.

We accompanied her to the back of the house. There she climbed on her bicycle and vanished silently down the back road.

"Well," said Woof to me as we walked back to the car, "tomorrow Dr Modi can go over and meet the dancing ghost. I'm looking forward to the rest of the fee. We'll buy you a warm rug for cold nights to be spent in the car waiting for ghosts!"

As Woof was about to get into the car, I gave a little growl. He had forgotten something. He looked at me in puzzlement and asked, "What is it?"

I trotted back to the tennis court and picked up the severed head.

"A papier-mache John the Baptist," Woof said and chuckling

he placed it on the seat beside him in the car.

He telephoned her the next day and told her we had the mask. She was quite happy to let us keep it.

It was my trophy. But don't ask me what Wuff thought when Woof hung it up on the wall!

10

The Case of the Human Bones

*P*erhaps the most difficult and irritating case I've ever had to work on was the Case of the Human Bones. What was particularly annoying was that, for a number of days, the humans around me didn't even realise that a crime had been committed. But I knew that a murder had taken place and the victim had been walking around only two weeks before, happily using these very bones which I was now bringing out, one by one, from their resting place under a thick bush deep in the jungle.

And yet it wasn't really very deep in the jungle; it was merely a place difficult of access. Even that is not a correct description of it, for the bush under which I found the bones grew at a junction of three footpaths. One of these footpaths came steeply down from a Moslem graveyard and the other two were deceptive for they led nowhere, ending suddenly in dense jungle. Those two footpaths were the kind that seem intended, wickedly, to make you lose your way; any innocent hiker proceeding along them was bound to find the walking so adventurous that having gone along so far, thrusting aside the thorny undergrowth, he would be tempted to struggle through a little further, thinking, no doubt, that somewhere ahead there must be a safer, easier continuation. Many years ago these paths probably did lead to some villages many miles away down in the valleys between the humps of many hills but now they were merely like the holding threads of a spider's web; they led you into a trap.

By sniffing at these paths I knew that the reason they still seemed usable was that buffaloes and cows and jackals and hyenas and wild boar travelled along them, treading part way and then, of course, moving off in any delicious direction. A human being going on along these paths would eventually have to crawl on all fours; other animals had made tunnels through the mass of thrusting, spindly branches. But even these green and brown tunnels floored with crackling dry leaves ended suddenly at some point in a knitted wall of jungle growth.

The entire murder episode centered round an ancient gold mine, the entrance to which was supposed to be hidden somewhere in the jungle. Babubhai, the victim, was not only an imaginative, ingenious man, he was also somewhat foolhardy. He was not really a local man; he had settled in these parts but he originally came from Gujarat, a neighbouring state. He had opened a general store in the Mahabaleshwar bazaar and he had prospered, but he was not much liked.

He was not a scrupulous man—he took advantage of people in any way he could. He was also something of a confidence trickster. The last trick he tried was to sell portions of the jungle which he owned at an exorbitant profit by making people believe that they had stumbled onto the hidden entrance to the lost gold mine. Many years before, he had bought ten acres of this hilly land but the seasonal stream that used to flow down through the jungle had changed its course high up in the hills and he was left holding ten acres of rocky, overgrown, useless land. But D.D. Bhai, as he was known, was not a man to give up easily. He believed in making a profit at any cost, even if he had to cheat people. So he worked out an elaborate ruse.

Whenever he spotted a likely buyer, he would strike up an acquaintance with him and, being a shopkeeper, he would ingratiate himself with the man in any way he could. Then, on some suitable evening, he would pretend to be terribly agitated and worried. Finally he would, in strict confidence, confess to the man that it had become necessary for him to sell at least another acre of the invaluable land which he owned. Having sworn his acquaintance to secrecy, D.D. Bhai would then tell him that he was certain that there was an ancient gold mine in that hilly tract. He would show the man a small gold nugget and say, "You see, I once found the entrance to the mine and there were gold nuggets even on the ground! But I lost the map I had made and now I can't locate the place again. I'm forced to sell off the land now, acre by acre, and some day some lucky devil will find the mine and I shall curse my fate. What an unlucky man I am!"

In this way he would play on the sympathy and greed of his acquaintance. The acquaintance would offer to buy an acre of the land in order to help D.D. Bhai out of his difficulties, but before doing this, of course, he would casually ask to see the land. D.D. Bhai would take him there and once deep into the jungle he would, on some natural pretext, go off into the bushes for a while leaving his acquaintance sitting on a stone or standing about surveying the area. Then D.D. Bhai would watch his acquaintance hopefully from behind a screen of bushes. In a short while, the acquaintance would spot the mouth of a tunnel-like cave somewhat overgrown with bushes. Moving towards it, he would see the glint of a nugget which D.D. Bhai had planted there. He would pick it up and, certain that he had not been seen, he would pocket it. D.D. Bhai always made sure that the men he set out to tempt in this manner were as dishonest and insincere as he was. None of them ever showed him the nugget they had found.

In this manner, he had managed to sell off, at various times, four acres of his land at more than a hundred per cent profit.

But the fifth man he duped turned out to be a hot-tempered,

vengeful person named Garud Sinh. He was not rich enough to sustain the loss of the money he had spent on buying the acre of land. In fact, he had sold or mortgaged everything he owned in order to purchase it. He talked to D.D. Bhai but the cheat would not return his money. Instead, D.D. Bhai said, "I didn't promise you a gold mine. It's your bad luck that you didn't find one on the land you bought. Now leave me alone and don't threaten me or I shall go to the police."

Garud Sinh left him alone. But he worked out a plan of his own. He sent his brother to D.D. Bhai, under an assumed name. Eventually, D.D. Bhai tried to sell the brother an acre of the land, too. The brother said to D.D. Bhai that if he liked the land—and frankly if he thought there was any hope of finding gold on that acre he would buy it at any price—D.D. Bhai would have to accompany him to Bombay since he had a large amount of cash there. He was prepared to close the deal that very night, if he was satisfied with the land and if D.D. Bhai came to Bombay to collect the money. D.D. Bhai was delighted. He wanted nothing more than to close the deal as soon as possible. He agreed, and giving the shop over to the charge of an assistant, announced to everyone concerned that he was likely to leave that evening for Bombay. D.D. Bhai was a secretive sort, especially where such dealings were concerned, and, of course, it was not uncommon for a shopkeeper to be away in Bombay for days on end.

So, when I found the bones of the murdered D.D. Bhai, no one connected them with the shopkeeper who was still supposed to be in Bombay.

As I say, this was perhaps the most difficult and irritating case I've had to work on so far. When I found the bones, I didn't have any idea of the complications that lay behind the crime. And even the little bit that I knew instinctively—that is, that a murder had taken place—was not believed. Of course, Woof was startled when I laid the bones before him at the junction of the three paths, but at first he thought they belonged to some sick or wounded wild animal which had crept into the bushes and died.

Then, when he realised they were human bones, he went up to the Moslem cemetery and, on enquiring, was told that it was possible that hyenas and jackals had got at some shallow grave. Another possibility was that gravediggers had thrown away old bones in order to make space for a new burial. Such things happened sometimes. To make matters worse, since the bones had been chewed clean by jackals they looked as though they had come out of some worm-eaten coffin. In any case, it was a horrifying mound of evidence to contemplate and Woof decided that we should go home and forget about it.

But we couldn't. I kept giving little barks all night and, sleeping under Woof's bed, I whined and moaned and Woof kept telling me to shut up, thinking I was having nightmares. He couldn't sleep properly either.

The next morning, Woof had a severe headache and he stopped by at the little consulting room of the local doctor. While chatting with the doctor, Woof told him about my find of the day before and how it was preying on his mind.

"You see, Dr Rao," Woof said, "Ranjha is not the sort of dog to go nosing about old bones. There must be hundreds in the jungle but he's never before brought them out and laid them in a little pile. I just can't stop worrying about it."

"Well," said Dr Rao, pushing his spectacles back on his nose and putting away his stethoscope, "there's no rush of patients today. So I might as well go along with you and examine the bones and set your mind at rest. That's modern medical science for you—cure a headache by removing its cause."

The doctor insisted we drive there in his rickety old Morris Minor. It had only two doors. A front seat was folded over and I climbed into the back. As we bumped over the rough roads, the doctor talked knowledgeably of the birds and trees we saw. He became so enthusiastic about nature's beauty that he had to swerve a number of times to keep to the road. I was buffeted about in the back. If I sat up, my head banged against the roof. If I lay down, the smell of the medicines in the little bottles

rolling about on the floor overcame me and I had to sit up again and shove my nose out of a front window.

"What's the matter with him?" the doctor asked gaily. "Can't he sit still? Shall I give him a sedative?"

Woof laughed and said, "Drive on, Doc. He's just excited by the grandeur of nature."

"Ah," said the doctor, and swerved again.

By the time we reached the cemetery I was so wobbly on my legs and weak in my stomach that I had first to attend to a number of little bushes.

"There, you see," said the doctor triumphantly. "He's not at all concerned about some rotting old bones."

But I was.

When we reached the pile, which was still there undisturbed, I went straight into the undergrowth and this time I moved off in a wider circle. All at once I caught the strong scent of the dead man's clothes. But search as I might, I couldn't find them. I looked up into the branches of trees as I had been taught to do and couldn't see them anywhere. Yet the smell of the dead man and of dried blood was very strong. I returned to Woof.

The doctor was down on one knee examining the bones. His face had grown very serious indeed.

At last he said, "These bones have been gnawed at by animals but I can say definitely that this man was alive less than two weeks ago. Of course, it *is* possible that they were removed from one of the recent graves by some wild animals but . . . I think we should inform the police."

I gave a bark and moved back and forth towards the bushes. Even the doctor understood my meaning.

He said, "I think he wants us to follow him."

I barked a little more. The doctor couldn't see how they were going to follow me into that tangle of bushes.

Woof broke off the slender overhanging branch of a tree and using that to push the brambles aside, came after me. The doctor followed in his wake.

At the spot where the smell of the clothes was strongest I started barking and sniffing about furiously.

The doctor's good humour had returned. He said, "I think the poor animal's gone hysterical."

Woof didn't say anything but followed me inch by inch as I sniffed.

Just then, a Russell's Viper slithered out from under a large stone and squirmed away into the bushes.

"Hey!" shouted the doctor. "That's a poisonous snake. That's probably what killed the man. The dog will get us all killed. He is after that snake. Call him off! Call him off, I tell you, or we'll be dead in minutes! Let's go back!"

So back we went. The doctor drove carefully all the way to the police station. He didn't talk of the birds and the trees. He just muttered, "That's a damned dangerous snake!"

Woof and the doctor both made statements to the police and then we left.

The next day we dropped in on the doctor. Woof said, "Well, Doc, the police don't seem to have come up with anything yet. They haven't got in touch as they said they would."

"No, they haven't. But it's too soon yet. Give them time. I'm sure they'll kill that snake if nothing else."

"Surely, Doc, you don't really think it was the snake's doing. The snake wouldn't carry the corpse and hide it in such dense growth. If the snake had done it, the body would have remained, bones and all, on the path."

"Yes." The doctor sighed, took off his spectacles, wiped his perspiring hands with a handkerchief, cleaned his glasses and replaced them on his nose. "Yes, I've been worrying about it, too. God, what a headache I have!"

Another day passed. Another night of bad dreams for me. I knew I had caught the scent of the dead man's clothes. I knew I should have persisted. But how could I when Woof had called me off? My first principle is obedience to him. I couldn't have done anything else and yet I felt I was failing in my duty as a detective dog. A scent is as clear to me as the sound of a bell to a human being. I wondered what Tughlak would have advised in the circumstances. Should I have refused to leave that spot?

On the third day, Dr Rao and Woof and I went to the police station. The agony of waiting was too much for us. And we were all suffering from those terrible headaches. The Inspector on duty was a friend of Woof's. He ordered tea and gave me a biscuit which, of course, I wouldn't touch till Woof told me to go ahead and eat. Woof was impatient. So was Dr Rao.

"Wait a bit," said the Inspector. "I have something to show you that'll be a relief to you."

In a while, a constable brought in a covered basket. Inside it was the Russell's Viper. The basket was tied all round with a cord.

"Don't open it," the Inspector said. "The snake is alive. Caught by some specialists. Plenty of snake-charmers around for this job. Good men. They'll earn something from the snake too. It's being sent off to the Haffkine Institute in Bombay. The venom is extracted, you know, and used for . . . what's the phrase, doctor?"

"Polyvalent anti-venin and other medicines."

"That's right. So, you see, that's that." The Inspector sipped his tea. The constable took the basket away. After a while, the Inspector frowned and said, "But, I must confess, a few things still worry me. Firstly, the snake-catchers tell me that the snake's pouch is still so full of venom that it seems he couldn't have killed a man in the last fortnight. Of course, most people don't die of the poison, they die of fright and shock. So it's still possible that the snake was responsible. But the second problem is, who was that man? No one has been reported missing. Could it be a casual visitor to the place or a wandering beggar perhaps? We haven't a clue. Of course, we're going through the usual procedures—having the dentures examined and so on—but the analysis will take some time. Meanwhile, it's a bit of a bother to think that there may be a murderer or murderers around. We hardly ever have any major crimes in this area. What's more, I'm due to go on transfer next week and I don't like to leave behind something like this unsolved . . ."

He trailed off and clutched briefly at the bridge of his nose. The doctor noticed the action and immediately brought a couple of tablets out of his pocket.

"Here, Inspector, these will relieve you."

"Thank you, doctor. I'm glad you carry them around in your pocket."

"Not normally," the doctor said with a feeble grin. "It's just that I have this awful headache myself." Then he laughed and looked at Woof and added, "I would never have believed a headache could be contagious."

So now, accompanied by the Inspector, we all went off to the spot where the bones had been found.

As before, I led them to the place where the smell of blood and clothes was strongest. But it had grown fainter. In a few days it would elude me completely. I knew I had to track down the source of the smell *now*. If I failed, perhaps the whole matter would be written off and even Woof might begin to think that the victim had merely met with an accident. His faith in my ability as a detective dog would be shattered, for surely he knew I was so agitated because I suspected that a crime had taken place.

This time the doctor was quiet and stepped about gingerly. He did not disturb my concentration as I worked. Perhaps he hoped that my success in the mission would help to cure his headache!

The Inspector and Woof were searching the bushes with the aid of sticks. They were obviously hoping to turn up some kind of evidence.

For me, the concentration of the scent in one spot was so annoying that I jumped up a number of times and then tried to remain standing on my hindlegs in order to test the air. Was the smell somehow falling from above? No, the air above was clean; the smell was strongest close to the ground and seemed to come from the earth.

Then it struck me. The blood-stained clothes had been buried!

I pawed at the earth. The criminals had been in a hurry. The clothes were quite near the surface. Soon I had the corner of a grey cotton jacket between my teeth. I pulled and tugged it free, almost falling over backwards in the attempt.

Woof and Dr Rao and the Inspector were astounded. Woof asked me to stand back and the Inspector carefully dug up the rest of the clothes.

After that, identifying the victim was not difficult. The police had the *dhobi* marks and laundry marks checked; the clothes were discovered to belong to D.D. Bhai. His family and shop assistants now knew that he had never reached Bombay. But, though they racked their brains, they couldn't provide any clue as to who the murderer could be.

Back we went to the jungle, and this time I was leading a police party. But the scent of the murderers had faded above ground though I had caught a bit of it on the clothes of the dead man.

Now I began to quarter the jungle, pushing through narrow tunnels of intermeshed branches and foliage. It was tough going for the policemen but they followed gamely. Everyone was scratched and bleeding and cursing. Then Woof called a halt.

"This is crazy!" he said. "We're not on a definite track and we're going to exhaust ourselves trying to keep pace with the dog. Let's wait here in this clearing and let the dog inform us when he's found something."

So they sat there and waited. Woof gave me the commands, "Ranjha—search, quarter, speak," and I bounded off.

An hour later, and more than a mile away, I came across the ashes of a fire that had been lit over three stones in a little clearing. A few yards from the fire, in the shrubbery, was a knife with dried blood on it. I sniffed at the blood. Yes, it was the same as that on the clothes I had found.

I barked.

Further up on the hillside, Woof and the police party could

hear the sound as it echoed up from somewhere in the valley. I must have barked more or less continuously for about ten minutes. But my ears told me clearly that the party was crashing off in the wrong direction. The echo was deceiving them.

I raced back to Woof. The party turned round and followed me.

Some of these men had been sent up on special detail from the district headquarters in Satara. One of them carried a walkie-talkie set that could communicate with the police van parked at the cemetery. When we reached the clearing, he informed the people in the van that we had found the knife and would try now to press on after the murderer or murderers. The van, of course, relayed this message on to the police station. In a while, we were told that some gold dust had been found in one of the pockets of the dead man's jacket.

No one touched the knife. Woof asked me to take the scent from its handle, which I did. But a two-week-old trail is difficult to follow. I frequently lost the scent. Eventually, I couldn't find it at all.

The head of the police party studied a pocket compass carefully and said, "You know, I think for a while they must have lost their way. That seems pretty clear from the manner in which they meandered about and had to stop for the night and light a fire in that clearing."

"Hm, very likely." Woof nodded. "But why do you say 'they' had lost their way? How are you so sure that there was more than one man?"

"Well, I noticed that three spots had been cleared of leaves. One was obviously for the fire and there were two other cleared areas in front of it. There must have been at least two men. I looked for footprints but the ground was dry. Also, I think these are not villagers but city men."

"Why do you think that? I must say you're making some very clever deductions."

The policeman laughed, and said modestly, "I used to be a

game scout, sir, and then I joined the Forest Department. I had plenty of experience catching poachers before joining the police."

"But why do you say these are city men?"

"I can't be absolutely sure, sir, but I am inclined to suppose it because, normally, a tired villager from these parts wouldn't trouble himself to sweep an area clean before sitting or lying down. You must have noted the broken, leafy sapling on one side of the fire. They used that to brush the leaves aside. What's more, an anxious villager would move straight through the jungle, in a downward direction, to the valley. After all, the valley provides the one sure way of escape. But these men have been following overgrown paths and have often moved parallel or away from the valley."

"Excellent!" Woof exclaimed delightedly. "If you don't mind my saying so, I'm sure you'll do very well in the police force."

"Thank you, sir. Very kind of you to say so. Might I make a suggestion?"

"Of course. You're in charge of the party."

"Well sir, it'll be dark soon and there's no further point in trying to track them through the jungle. Let's go back to the van and drive to the villages in the valley. We can make inquiries there about any strangers who may have emerged from the jungle about two weeks ago."

"Right," said Woof and back we all went to the van and the other vehicles parked there.

In the villages of the valley, however, we drew a blank. Finally we stopped at a roadside stall for some refreshment.

"Well?" Woof asked turning to the head of the party. "What shall we do now? There's not a clue to the identity of these two men."

"Oh, but there is, sir."

Woof looked at the man in astonishment. "There is?"

"Yes, sir. The very fact that the villagers don't consider these men strangers means that they are familiar sights in this region. But, as I said, they are city men. So our next step should be to find out who are the city men who are often seen in this area. Even buses don't come to these villages. So these men are either some kind of traders or they have settled here recently. We've radioed a message to the Inspector and he'll be meeting us here shortly with a list of such men."

When the Inspector arrived, he clapped the clever policeman on his shoulder and said, "Good work, Havildar Kamble!" A *havildar* is a constable in the Indian Police Service.

Havildar Kamble saluted and said, "Thank you, sir." Then he patted me as I stood beside him and added, "But it was Ranjha who provided all the clues."

"Yes, that's true, and I shan't forget it," said the Inspector.

As we went from house to house checking on the new residents of the area, I was able to provide one more clue.

Towards midnight, we knocked on the door of Garud Sinh. As he opened the door, the faint scent I had caught on the knife-handle now struck me with full force. I leapt at him. Startled and frightened, he fell over. I took his wrist in my mouth.

"That's your man, Inspector!" Woof shouted in excitement.

The police were more calm about it. They were used to catching murderers and meeting them face to face. Also, evidence provided by a tracker dog is not enough to convict a man in court.

The Inspector had come prepared with search warrants. The police searched the house. Of course, they found the title deed to the land and that was no surprise since they already knew about the sales which D.D. Bhai had made. But then they found the gold nugget.

When Garud Sinh was confronted with the fact that gold dust from the same nugget had been found in the pocket of the dead man's jacket, he broke down and confessed. He was a proud man. He cried out that he didn't want to be hanged as a thief. He had never stooped to thievery. He had only avenged himself against the man who had cheated him.

Garud Sinh's brother had fled to Bombay soon after their

return to the village. Within hours of receiving a message to this effect, the Bombay police arrested the man.

In a few weeks, the case came up in court. I had to make an appearance; the judge was curious to see me. In a few minutes Woof led me out again. I didn't have to say or do anything! But I couldn't help growling when I saw Garud Sinh in the dock.

Later, when I heard Dr Rao and Woof discussing the case, I learnt that the judge had been pleased enough to commend me for the help I had rendered. The criminals were given life imprisonment.

And, true to his word, the Inspector hadn't forgotten me. He presented me a feeding bowl on behalf of the entire police party. It was actually a helmet of the Riot Police. It had a plaque on it which Woof read out to me. It said: *To Dog Detective Ranjha from his friends, the police.*

11

The Case of the Superstitious Gardener

*I*n the weeks that followed the solution of the Case of the Human Bones, Dr Rao and Woof often talked about it, but one thing that irritated the doctor was the title we had given it. He preferred to call it the Case of the Gold Nugget. He complained that the very mention of the human bones which had led to the discovery of the crime gave him the beginnings of a headache.

So too, in this case. The gardener concerned would not have liked the title for he didn't think he was superstitious at all. He thought he was behaving in a rational, reasonable, normal way. But, of course, he *was* superstitious.

Actually, this was not a very serious case. In fact, it turned out to be something of a joke and the only reason I recall it here is because it shows how gullible human beings can be.

The gardener was known as Bhau Malli. He looked so typically the yokel—with his teeth spraying outwards over his lower lip, his stammer, his over-emphatic gestures and his little white

cap set aslant on the back of his head—that people usually refused to think that he was as foolish as he looked. Such a stupid-
looking man, they said, must be intelligent; God has ways of
hiding His light under a bushel. Bhau Malli must be quite clever
under his camouflage. And, indeed, everything seemed to verify
that assessment.

Bhau Malli's garden flourished. He rarely watered the plants
and when he did, it was always under the noonday sun. But
flowers sprouted and birds chirped about and bees made honey-
combs in the trees. Bhau Malli lived like a happy jungle savage
in that garden. He never even cut the grass but it never grew too
long because wandering cattle and donkeys sauntered in and
chewed it trim. The house and garden were enclosed by gates, of
course. But Bhau Malli never shut the gates. Instead, he charged
a fee of anyone whose cattle had fed in his grounds. People
marvelled at his ability to prosper and to smile through all ad-
versity—which he actually seemed to invite—while other gardeners were clutching their turbans and running about chucking
stones at intruding monkeys and such. Bhau Malli gave bananas
and nuts to the visiting hordes of monkeys, and sometimes he
pretended he could discuss things with them. When you consider it carefully, perhaps it was not such a silly thing for him to
do because otherwise he would just stand there in the garden
and talk to himself.

Bhau Malli had a family. He had a wife and five children.
Some of the children looked like him and some of them didn't. It
is possible that one or two of them had just wandered in through
the open gate and joined the brood. Anything was possible. For
instance, various dogs slipped into the garden and within minutes became his. There was one lame creature who barked and
snarled at nothing, somewhat like his master, and when he was
carted away one day by a man who claimed him, the mangy dog
limped back a year later from a village one hundred miles away.

If a bitch littered in some cosy corner of the sprawling garden,
Bhau Malli sold the sweet little pups and with the money held a

little feast and invited a local pundit to hold a prayer meeting in his hut. The mother of the pups would go sniffing after the pups and, within the week, they would come, toddling one by one behind her, back into the garden. Sometimes he sold the same pups three times over.

There were days, too, when he would tuck a flower behind his ear and declare it a holiday and go to sleep under a tree. If some neighbour's hens disturbed him with their furious clucking, he would bestir himself to go and pick up the eggs they had laid. He always drank milk in the evenings, drawn straight from the udders of visiting cows. And he never bothered to lop the dead wood from trees in the garden. Instead, he sold parts of trees by the branch to local woodcutters.

The owner of the house suspected most of this but being a kind old lady who lived most of the time in Poona, she let Bhau Malli drift on his ways as long as the garden was kept well. And it was. On the rare occasions when she had reason to pull him up, he would look up at the sky and mutter at God for not letting the rains fall. His manner seemed to imply that she would do better to take the matter up with Higher Authority; it was beyond his control.

Most people would have thought that this was a clever ruse on the part of the gardener but the fact is he was quite sincere.

One day Bhau Malli came to Woof and asked for a contribution of ten rupees; he said he was raising money in order to engage the services of a holy man who would entreat God on his behalf and help him to recover some pots which had been stolen from his hut. Now, Woof knew that Bhau Malli was a devout Hindu and given to practising the occasional ritual. He was therefore pleasantly surprised and pleased to discover that Bhau Malli was, in addition, a broadminded man who believed in the good of all religions. For it was Bhau Malli's intention to go to a Moslem holy man in the bazaar who, it was said, could, by opening the Koran at random, divine the truth of many mysteries. The holy man had a reputation for solving crimes by divination.

But while Woof was delighted with Bhau Malli's reverence for beliefs other than his own, Woof was shocked that he was so superstitious as to think that the mumbo-jumbo of a charlatan could help him get back his stolen pots and pans.

Woof said, "I don't mind contributing ten rupees towards the recovery of your stolen utensils but, in my opinion, you would be much better served if you depended on this dog to help you. I suggest you save your money—and, incidentally, mine—and forget about going to the holy man. Tell me how the pots came to be stolen and I'm sure Ranjha will prove of more use to you than the holy man."

Bhau Malli took Woof's chiding in good spirit; he laughed and grinned and nodded and seemed to agree but, in the end, he insisted on going to the holy man.

"Very well," said Woof. "Let us see who catches the thief, Ranjha or the holy man."

When Bhau returned from his visit to the holy man, Woof asked what had transpired. Bhau said that the holy man was working on the case with his mystic vision but in the meantime he had admitted that it was all a bit foggy. Sooner or later, the mist over the matter was bound to clear.

"Good heavens!" Woof exclaimed. "That's as vague as any man can be."

Bhau nodded and grinned and sucked in his breath and with an emphatic gesture said, "Yes, very, very vague. B-b-b-but he's w-w-w-working on the c-c-case. He's told me not to w-w-worry."

"All right," Woof said. "Now let me put Ranjha into his tracking harness and let's go over to your hut."

The pots had been stolen three days before, on Republic Day, when the whole family had gone to the bazaar to join in the anniversary festivities and to watch the parade. Bhau's hut, like the gate to the garden, was never locked. The door had been left ajar. The thief had strolled in, seen that he was unobserved, and selected the best copper pots from the shelf and walked away.

Bhau Malli was particularly upset for the pots had been his very special ones, the ones made of copper. The brass and stainless steel utensils had not been touched. The thief, it seemed, had the same values as Bhau Malli—he, too, had a preference for copper vessels. This in itself was a surprise to Woof for copper pots are not half as durable as those made of the popular alloys, but Bhau Malli explained that copper was considered a metal of magical properties and had a curative value and, therefore, it was quite understandable that the thief had made such a careful selection. What's more, last year, too, a similar theft had taken place but then Bhau had not bothered much about it since only one copper mug had been stolen. He had, in fact, eventually come to believe that one of his five children had misplaced it somewhere in the vast reaches of the garden. Now, Bhau knew that he was the target of a thief, for this time six utensils had been taken.

Three days had now passed since the theft. Woof was a little doubtful that I would be able to untangle the scent of the thief from all those of the family and the various genuine visitors who had been there in the past few days. Bhau was of the opinion that one of his own relatives, in particular perhaps a young niece, had carried the pots away in a shopping bag. On that Republic Day, many of his relatives had come from the surrounding villages.

Woof groaned at the thought of tracking through the crowded bazaar and perhaps following a trail to some remote village.

But he needn't have worried. The trail led right across the road to the hotel opposite.

Yes, I caught the unfamiliar scent straightaway. Of course, the hut itself was full of numerous smells, some of them strange and obviously belonging to the relatives who had been there; but none of them had had reason to stand directly under the shelf from which the pots had been taken. There, under the shelf, I detected only one strange scent—that of the man who had reached up for the pots. It was Woof who deduced this and it was he who pointed me to the exact spot and set me on the track. After all my training and having solved so many cases, Woof and I had become quite a good working team. I understood what he wanted of me. And he was thrilled by my immediate response.

I set off slowly towards the main gate, with my nose to the ground. But at one point, the scent suddenly veered to the left. Following it, I came to the edge of the compound and a large rainwater pit that lay just beyond the straggling fence. The thief had been sensible; he had not carried the pots out of the compound for fear of being noticed—he had thrown his booty over the fence and collected it later. However, I didn't go sniffing off after the smell of the pots. The scent I had been given was that of the thief and I kept to it.

It turned back towards the drive and went out of the main gate and, as I said, across the road, through a side entrance into the vast grounds of an hotel. The man had gone to   broom and continued sweeping the dried leaves into little heaps all over the compound. I naturally moved from heap to heap. In a short while, Woof understood that the man I was tracking was a sweeper, an employee of the hotel.

When Woof mentioned this to Bhau, he said, "But there are many sweepers employed by the hotel."

So I pressed on, till I reached the hut of this particular sweeper at the back of the main building. A woman and some children standing there moved aside at my approach. I led Woof and Bhau into the hut. There, lined neatly in row upon row on shelves, were many gleaming pots and pans. There were rows of crockery and glassware too. The man was obviously a specialist—specialising in the theft of kitchenware. But there was no sign of Bhau's goods. Again, the thief had been sensible. He had not put them out on display so soon after acquiring them. They were probably hidden somewhere safe. Or perhaps they had been sold.

Woof asked the woman where her husband was. She said he had gone to the bazaar.

Woof now took me off the scent and turned to Bhau. He said,

"So there you are. It's clear that the man who lives in this hut stole your pots. He might have sold them by now, of course, but I doubt it. He seems to like possessing copper pots. He's probably hidden them somewhere and, if we went on tracking, I'm sure we'd find them but I don't think it's necessary to take all that trouble. I suggest you see the sweeper later this evening and just tell him casually that we know who the thief is. Tell him that you are only interested in getting your pots back and, if they are returned to you, nothing more will be said of the matter; otherwise, of course, you will have no alternative but to expose the thief. I'm sure you'll get your pots back."

Bhau sucked in his breath, nodded eagerly and said, "Yes, yes." Then his face fell in dismay and he added, "B-b-but that sweeper is such a nice man. I know him w-w-well."

"I understand that. I realised you'd know him. After all, he's a neighbourhood employee. That's why I suggest you merely talk to him without causing too much fuss. Otherwise, the man will, to say the least, lose his job, for I'm certain the hotel won't continue to employ him once we've proved his guilt."

Two days later, Woof met Bhau.

Bhau waved a sort of salute, grinned and said, "I went to the h-h-h-holy man."

"Again?"

Bhau nodded. "He said I was going to get my pots b-b-back. He said the m-m-man who stole them lives in the same neighbourhood."

"Did you tell him that we had tracked the man?"

"Of c-c-course."

Woof shook his head and sighed. "Bhau, you're impossible! If you've told the holy man all that we did, he's naturally going to say that you'll get the pots back!"

"It's not like that," Bhau said, then added sagely, "he knows."

"And have you told the sweeper that you know who the thief is?"

Bhau shifted uneasily on his feet and looked down. At last, he shook his head. "He's a n-n-n-nice man. How c-c-can I say such things to him?"

"Then," said Woof bluntly, "I'm afraid you'll never get your pots back. You can forget about them."

Bhau said simply and with finality, "The holy m-m-man said I would get them back."

The days passed. Nothing happened. There was no sign of the missing pots. Bhau's wife could bear it no longer. She marched up to the sweeper and told him that we knew who the thief was; he admitted casually that his wife had told him about the dog that came tracking to his door.

The next morning the pots were found thrown about outside Bhau's hut. Someone had flung them in over the fence the previous night.

Bhau's wife came to Woof and informed him. When we got there Bhau was standing among his children, gaping with joy at the pots.

"Come on, Bhau, there's a little bit of proving still left to be done."

Bhau looked at Woof and said, "God has given me b-b-back the pots."

"Right," said Woof, "so let's go and meet God's agent."

And saying that, he asked me to take the scent from the pots. The sweeper's smell sizzled up my nose as strong as the odour of cowdung and as heady as Egyptian perfume. I searched the ground in widening circles till I caught the beginning of the trail. I crawled under the fence. Woof asked me to wait and I did till he and Bhau came round through the gate. Then I took them, as straight as the flight of an arrow, to the sweeper's hut. He was standing by the door but seeing us coming, he stepped inside quickly and shut the door. Woof called out to me to stop.

Then he turned to Bhau. "Is that proof enough for you? He's the man who threw those pots in during the night."

Bhau moved his head in a semicircular, sideways movement. It was a gesture indicating agreement.

But in the afternoon Bhau came to Woof and said, "Everyone has given me some money. I'm making a c-c-collection."

"For what?"

"B-b-b-because I got my pots b-b-back."

"Oh," said Woof with a smile, "you needn't buy anything for Ranjha. He likes helping friends."

"It's not for the d-d-dog," Bhau said. "It's to thank God. It's for the holy man. He was right after all. I did get my pots b-b-back."

And so, to this day, in the vast garden of the bungalow opposite that hotel, you may see a gardener named Bhau Malli happily going about his chores, with a flower tucked behind his ear. Sometimes he will stop to pick up a hen's egg or pluck a berry that's ripe enough to eat. Sometimes he will talk to passing monkeys and sometimes he will stand, with his cap aslant on his head, talking to himself. If you listen closely, you might hear him muttering, "Yes, f-f-faith is the most important thing on earth."

And who is there to prove him wrong?

12

Tughlak Sums It Up

I was now well-known all over Mahabaleshwar. Children would stop by on their way back from school to play games with me or accompany us for a walk. Adults would point me out to visitors as we went by. But I must say that despite all the fine things said to me during this early part of my career, none touched me as much as the way in which Tughlak greeted me when we returned to Bombay.

He ambled up to me in the centre of the racecourse, cocking his head from side to side all the while. I knew he was sizing me up. Then he wagged his tail. He didn't address me as "boy" even though I still couldn't have worked up the courage to call him just plain Tughlak.

He said, "Hello there, Old Toot! It's good to have you back."

Old Toot!

I could have sung it and danced it all over the place. Tughlak had called me Old Toot!

I knew now for certain that I was no longer a pup.

I was grown-up.